THE BIG SUN OF MERCURY

The Big Sun of Mercury

Isaac Asimov

NEW ENGLISH LIBRARY
TIMES MIRROR

The Big Sun of Mercury first published in 1956 by Doubleday
under the title of Lucky Starr And The Big Sun of Mercury by Paul French
© 1956 by Doubleday & Co. Inc. Forward © Isaac Asimov 1972
First published in Great Britain in 1973, by New English Library

*

FIRST NEL PAPERBACK EDITION MARCH 1974
This New Edition October 1974

*

NEL Books are published by The New English Library Limited from Barnard's Inn,
Holborn, London E.C.1. Made and printed in Great Britain by C. Nicholls & Company
Ltd.

45001767 2

To ROBYN JOAN,
who did her best to interfere.

CONTENTS

FOREWORD

THIS BOOK WAS FIRST PUBLISHED IN 1956, and the description of the surface of Mercury was in accordance with astronomic beliefs of the period.

Since 1956, however, astronomical knowledge of the inner Solar system has advanced enormously because of the use of radar beams and rockets.

In 1956, it had been thought that Mercury always faced one side to the Sun, so that there was a portion that was perpetually in sunlight and a portion that was perpetually dark, with some boundary regions which sometimes had Sun and sometimes not.

In 1965, however, astronomers studied radar-beam reflections from the surface of Mercury and found, to their surprise, that this was not so. Whereas Mercury revolved about the Sun in 88 days, it rotated on its axis in 59 days. This meant that every part of Mercury was exposed to the Sun at one time or another and there was no "dark side" after all.

I hope that the readers enjoy this story anyway, but I would not wish them to be misguided into accepting as fact some of the material which was "accurate" in 1956 but which is now outdated.

ISAAC ASIMOV
November, 1970

1

THE GHOSTS OF THE SUN

LUCKY STARR AND HIS SMALL FRIEND, John Bigman Jones, followed the young engineer up the ramp toward the air lock that led to the surface of the planet Mercury.

Lucky thought: At least things are breaking fast.

He had been on Mercury only an hour. He had had scarcely time to do more than see his ship, the *Shooting Starr,* safely stowed in the underground hangar. He had met only the technicians who had handled the landing red tape and seen to his ship.

Those technicians, that is, and Scott Mindes, engineer in charge of Project Light. It had been almost as though the young man had been lying in wait. Almost at once he had suggested a trip to the surface.

To see some of the sights, he had explained.

Lucky did not believe that, of course. The engineer's small-chinned face had been haunted with trouble, and his mouth twitched as he spoke. His eyes slid away from Lucky's cool, level glance.

Yet Lucky agreed to visit the surface. As yet, all he knew of the troubles on Mercury was that they posed a ticklish problem for the Council of Science. He was willing to go along with Mindes and see where that led him.

As for Bigman Jones, he was always glad to follow Lucky anywhere and any time, for any reason and no reason.

But it was Bigman whose eyebrows lifted as all three were getting into their suits. He nodded almost unnoticeably toward the holster attachment on Mindes's suit.

Lucky nodded calmly in return. He, too, had noticed that protruding from the holster was the butt of a heavy-caliber blaster.

The young engineer stepped out onto the surface of the planet first. Lucky Starr followed and Bigman came last.

For the moment, they lost contact with one another in the nearly total darkness. Only the stars were visible, bright and hard in the cold airlessness.

Bigman recovered first. The gravity here on Mercury was almost exactly equal to that on his native Mars. The Martian nights were almost as dark. The stars in its night sky were almost as brilliant.

His treble voice sounded brightly in the receivers of the others. "Hey, I'm beginning to make things out."

So was Lucky, and the fact puzzled him. Surely starlight could not be *that* bright. There was a faint, luminous haze that lay over the tumbled landscape and touched its sharp crags with a pale milkiness.

Lucky had seen something of the sort on the Moon during its two-week-long night. There, also, was the completely barren landscape, rough and broken. Never, in millions of years, either there on the Moon or here on Mercury, had there been the softening touch of wind or rain. The bare rock, colder than imagination could picture, lay without a touch of frost in a waterless world.

And in the Moon's night, too, there had been this milkiness. But there, over half the Moon at least, there had been Earth-light. When Earth was full it shone with sixteen times the brightness of the full Moon as seen from Earth.

Here on Mercury, at the Solar Observatory at the North Pole, there was no near-by planet to account for the light.

"Is that starlight?" he finally asked, knowing it wasn't.

Scott Mindes said wearily, "That's the coronal glimmer."

"Great Galaxy," said Lucky with a light laugh. "The corona! Of course! I should have known!"

"Known what?" cried Bigman. "What's going on? Hey, Mindes, come on, give!"

Mindes said, "Turn around. You've got your back to it."

They all turned. Lucky whistled softly between his teeth; Bigman yelped with surprise. Mindes said nothing.

A section of the horizon was etched sharply against a pearly region of the sky. Every pointed irregularity of that part of the horizon was in keen focus. Above it, the sky was in a soft glow (fading with height) a third of the way to the zenith. The glow consisted of bright, curving streamers of pale light.

"That's the corona, Mr. Jones," said Mindes.

Even in his astonishment Bigman was not forgetful of his own conception of the proprieties. He growled, "Call me Bigman." Then he said, "You mean the corona around the Sun? I didn't think it was that big."

"It's a million miles deep or more," said Mindes, "and we're on Mercury, the planet closest to the Sun. We're only thirty million miles from the Sun right now. You're from Mars, aren't you?"

"Born and bred," said Bigman.

"Well, if you could see the Sun right now, you'd find it was thirty-six times as big as it is when seen from Mars, and so's the corona. And thirty-six times as bright too."

Lucky nodded. Sun and corona would be nine times as large as seen from Earth. And the corona could not be seen at all on Earth, except during periods of total eclipse.

Well, Mindes had not altogether lied. There were sights to be seen on Mercury. He tried to fill out the corona, to imagine the Sun it surrounded which was now hidden just below the horizon. It would be a majestic sight!

Mindes went on, an unmistakable bitterness in his voice. "They call this light 'the white ghost of the Sun.' "

Lucky said, "I like that. A rather good phrase."

"Rather good?" said Mindes savagely. "I don't think so. There's too much talk about ghosts on this planet. This planet's all jinx. Nothing ever goes right on it. The mines failed . . ." His voice trailed off.

Lucky thought: We'll let that simmer.

Aloud he said, "Where is this phenomenon we were to see, Mindes?"

"Oh yes. We'll have to walk a bit. Not far, considering the gravity, but watch your footing. We don't have roads here, and the coronal glimmer can be awfully confusing. I suggest the helmet lights."

He clicked his on as he spoke, and a shaft of light sprang out from above the face-plate, turning the ground into a rough patchwork of yellow and black. Two other lights flashed on, and the three figures moved forward on their thickly insulated boots. They made no sound in the vacuum, but each could sense the soft vibrations set up by each footfall in the air within their suits.

Mindes seemed to be brooding about the planet as he walked. He said in a low, tense voice, "I hate Mercury. I've been here six months, two Mercurian years, and I'm sick of it. I didn't think I'd be here more than six months to begin with, and here the time's up and nothing's done. Nothing. Everything about this place is wrong. It's the smallest planet. It's the closest to the Sun. Only one side faces the Sun. Over there"—and his arm swung in the direction of the corona's gleam—"is the Sun-side, where it gets hot enough in places to melt lead and boil sulfur. Over there in the other direction"—again his arm swung—"is the one planetary surface in the whole Solar System that never sees the Sun. Everything about the place is miserable."

He paused to jump over a shallow, six-foot-wide rift

in the surface, a reminder of some eons-old Mercury-quake, perhaps, which could not heal over without wind and weather. He made the jump clumsily, the picture of an Earthman who, even on Mercury, stayed close to the artificial gravity of the Observatory Dome.

Bigman clicked his tongue disapprovingly at the sight. He and Lucky negotiated the jump with scarcely anything more than a lengthening of stride.

A quarter mile farther on, Mindes said abruptly, "We can see it from here, and just in time too."

He stopped, teetering forward, with arms outflung for balance. Bigman and Lucky halted with a small hop which kicked up a spurt of gravel.

Mindes's helmet flash went out. He was pointing. Lucky and Bigman put out their own lights and there, in the darkness, where Mindes had pointed, was a small, irregular splotch of white.

It was brilliant, a more burning sunshine than Lucky had ever seen on Earth.

"This is the best angle for seeing it," said Mindes. "It's the top of Black and White Mountain."

"Is that its name?" asked Bigman.

"That's right. You see why, don't you? It stands just far enough nightward of the Terminator——— That's the boundary between the dark-side and the Sun-side."

"I know that," said Bigman indignantly. "You think I'm ignorant?"

"I'm just explaining. There's this little spot around the North Pole, and another around the South Pole, where the Terminator doesn't move much as Mercury circles the sun. Down at the Equator, now, the Terminator moves seven hundred miles in one direction for forty-four days and then seven hundred miles back in the next forty-four. Here it just moves half a mile or so altogether, which is why this is a good place for an observatory. The Sun and the stars stand still.

"Anyway, Black and White Mountain is just far enough away so that only the top half of it is lit up at most. Then, as the Sun creeps away, the light moves up the mountain slopes."

"And now," interposed Lucky, "only the peak is lit up."

"Only the top foot or two maybe, and that will be gone soon. It will be all dark for an Earth-day or two, and then the light starts coming back."

Even as he spoke the white splotch shrank to a dot that burned like a bright star.

The three men waited.

"Look away," advised Mindes, "so that your eyes get accustomed to darkness."

And after slow minutes he said, "All right, look back."

Lucky and Bigman did so and for a while saw nothing.

And then it was as though the landscape had turned bloody. Or a piece of it had, at any rate. First there was just the sensation of redness. Then it could be made out; a rugged mountain climbing up to a peak. The peak was brightly red now, the red deepening and fading as the eye traveled downward until all was black.

"What is it?" asked Bigman.

"The Sun," said Mindes, "has sunk just low enough now so that, from the mountain peak, all that remains above the horizon is the corona and the prominences. The prominences are jets of hydrogen gas that lift thousand of miles above the Sun's surface, and they're a bright red in color. Their light is there all the time, but ordinary sunlight drowns it out."

Again Lucky nodded. The prominences were again something which on Earth could be seen only during a total eclipse or with special instruments, thanks to the atmosphere.

"In fact," added Mindes in a low voice, "they call this 'the red ghost of the Sun.' "

"That's two ghosts," said Lucky suddenly, "a white one and a red one. Is it because of the ghosts that you carry a blaster, Mr. Mindes?"

Mindes shouted, "What?" Then, wildly, "What are you talking about?"

"I'm saying," said Lucky, "that it's time you told us

why you really brought us out here. Not just for the sights, I'm sure, or you wouldn't carry a blaster on an empty, desolate planet."

It took a while for Mindes to answer. When he did, he said, "You're David Starr, aren't you?"

"That's right," said Lucky patiently.

"You're a member of the Council of Science. You're the man they call Lucky Starr."

Members of the Council of Science shunned publicity, and it was with a certain reluctance that Lucky said again, "That's right."

"Then I'm not wrong. You're one of their ace investigators, and you're here to investigate Project Light."

Lucky's lips thinned as they pressed together. He would much rather that were not so easily known. He said, "Maybe that's true, maybe it isn't. Why did you bring me here?"

"I know it's true, and I brought you here"—Mindes was panting—"to tell you the truth before the others could fill you—full of—lies."

"About what?"

"About the failures that have been haunting—I hate that word—the failures in Project Light."

"But you might have told me what you wanted to back at the Dome. Why bring me here?"

"For two reasons," said the engineer. His breathing continued rapid and difficult. "In the first place, they all think it's my fault. They think I can't pull the project through, that I'm wasting tax money. I wanted to get you away from them. Understand? I wanted to keep you from listening to them first."

"Why should they think it's your fault?"

"They think I'm too young."

"How old are you?"

"Twenty-two."

Lucky Starr, who wasn't very much older, said, "And your second reason?"

"I wanted you to get the feeling of Mercury. I wanted you to absorb the—the——" He fell silent.

Lucky's suited figure stood straight and tall on Mercury's forbidding surface, and the metal of one shoulder caught and reflected the milky light of the corona, "the white ghost of the Sun."

He said, "Very well, Mindes, suppose I accept your statement that you are not responsible for failures in the project. Who is?"

The engineer's voice was a vague mutter at first. It coalesced gradually into words. "I don't know—— At least——"

"I don't understand you," said Lucky.

"Look," said Mindes desperately, "I've investigated. I spent waking and sleeping periods trying to pinpoint the blame. I watched everybody's movements. I noted times when accidents took place, when there were breaks in the cables or when conversion plates were smashed. And one thing I'm sure of——"

"Which is?"

"That nobody at the Dome can be directly responsible. Nobody. There are only about fifty people in the Dome, fifty-two to be exact, and the last six times something has gone wrong I've been able to account for each one. Nobody was anywhere near the scenes of the accidents." His voice had gone high-pitched.

Lucky said, "Then how do you account for the accidents? Mercury-quakes? Action of the Sun?"

"Ghosts!" cried the engineer wildly, flinging his arms about. "There's a white ghost and a red ghost. You've seen those. But there are two-legged ghosts too. I've seen them, but will anyone believe me?" He was almost incoherent. "I tell you—— I tell you——"

Bigman said, "Ghosts! Are you nuts?"

At once Mindes screamed, "You don't believe me either. But I'll prove it. I'll blast the ghost. I'll blast the fools who won't believe me. I'll blast everyone. Everyone!"

With a harsh screech of laughter he had drawn his blaster, and with frenzied speed, before Bigman could move to stop him, he had aimed it at Lucky at point-blank range and squeezed its trigger. Its invisible field of disruption lashed out——

2

MAD OR SANE?

It would have been the end of Lucky if he and Mindes had been on Earth.

Lucky had not missed the gathering madness in Mindes's voice. He had been waiting carefully for some break, some action to suit the violence of the engineer's hard-breathed sentences. Yet he had not entirely expected an outright assault with the blaster.

When Mindes's hand flashed to his holster, Lucky leaped to one side. On Earth, that movement would have come too late.

On Mercury, however, matters were different. Mercury's gravity was two fifths that of Earth, and Lucky's contracting muscles threw his abnormally light body (even including the suit he wore) farther to one side. Mindes, unaccustomed to low gravity, stumbled as he turned too quickly in order that his blaster might follow Lucky's motion.

The blaster's energy, therefore, struck bare ground, inches from Lucky's sinking body. It gouged a foot-deep hole into the frigid rock.

Before Mindes could recover and aim again, Bigman had struck him at the end of a long, low tackle carried through with the natural grace of a born Martian accustomed to low gravity.

Mindes went down. He shrieked wordlessly and then was silent, whether unconscious as the result of the fall or as the climax of his fevered emotions could not be told.

Bigman did not believe either possibility. "He's shamming," he cried passionately. "The dirty cobber is playing dead." He had wrenched the blaster from the fallen engineer's unresisting grip, and now he pointed it at the man's head.

Lucky said sharply, "None of that, Bigman."

Bigman hesitated. "He tried to kill you, Lucky." It was obvious that the little Martian would not have been half as angry if it had merely been himself who had been in danger of death. Yet he backed away.

Lucky was on his knees examining Mindes's face through the face-plate, shining his helmet light onto the other's pale, drawn features. He checked the pressure gauge of Mindes's suit, making sure the shock of the fall had not loosened any of its joints. Then, seizing the fallen figure by a wrist and ankle, he slung it across his shoulders and rose to his feet.

"Back to the Dome," he said, "and, I'm afraid, to a problem that's a little more complicated than the Chief thinks."

Bigman grunted and followed Lucky's long stride closely, his own smaller build forcing him into a gravity-lengthened half trot. He kept his blaster ready, maneuvering his position to enable him, in case of need, to strike at Mindes without blasting down Lucky.

The "Chief" was Hector Conway, head of the Council of Science. At more informal times he was called Uncle Hector by Lucky, since it was Hector Conway, along with Augustus Henree, who were the guardians of the young Lucky after the death of Lucky's parents as the result of a pirate attack near the orbit of Venus.

A week earlier Conway had said to Lucky with a casual air, almost as though he were offering him a vacation, "How would you like to go to Mercury, Lucky?"

"What's up, Uncle Hector?" asked Lucky.

"Nothing really," said Conway, frowning, "except some cheap politics. We're supporting a rather expensive project up at Mercury, one of those basic research things that may come to nothing, you know, and, on the other hand, may turn out to be quite revolutionary. It's a gamble. All those things are."

Lucky said, "Is it anything I know about?"

"I don't think so. It's quite recent. Anyway, Senator Swenson has pounced on it as an example of how the Council wastes taxpayers' money. You know the line. He's pressing for an investigation, and one of his boys went out to Mercury some months ago."

"Senator Swenson? I see." Lucky nodded. This was nothing new. The Council of Science over the past decades had slowly come to the fore of the fight against the dangers to Earth from both within and without the Solar System. In this age of Galactic civilization, with humanity spread through all the planets of all the stars in the Milky Way, only scientists could properly cope with mankind's problems. In fact, only the specially trained scientists of the Council were adequate.

Yet there were some men of Earth's government who feared the growing power of this Council of Science and others who used this suspicion to further their own ambitions. Senator Swenson was the foremost of the latter group. His attacks, usually directed against the Council's "wasteful" way of supporting research, were making him famous.

Lucky said, "Who's the man in charge of the project on Mercury? Anyone I know?"

"It's called Project Light, by the way. And the man in charge is an engineer named Scott Mindes. A bright boy, but he's not the man to handle this. The most embarrassing thing is that since Swenson kicked up this fuss all sorts of things have been going wrong with Project Light."

"I'll look into it if you wish, Uncle Hector."

"Good. The accidents and bad breaks are nothing, I'm sure, but we don't want Swenson to maneuver us into some bad-looking spot. See what he's up to. And watch out for that man of his. Urteil is his name and he has a reputation of being a capable and dangerous fellow."

So that was all it started out as. Just a bit of investigation to forestall political difficulties. Nothing more.

Lucky landed on Mercury's North Pole expecting nothing more, and in two hours found himself at the wrong end of a blaster bolt.

Lucky thought as he slogged back to the Dome with Mindes over his shoulders: There's more than just a bit of politics here.

Dr. Karl Gardoma stepped out of the small hospital room and faced Lucky and Bigman somberly. He was wiping his strong hands on a pad of fluffy plastosorb, which he tossed into the disposal unit when he finished. His dark-complexioned face, almost brown, was disturbed, his heavy eyebrows lowering. Even his black hair, cut close so that it stood up stiffly in thick array, seemed to accentuate his troubled appearance.

"Well, Doctor?" said Lucky.

Dr. Gardoma said, "I've got him under sedation. He'll be all right when he wakes. I don't know if he'll remember clearly what happened."

"Has he had attacks like this before?"

"Not since he came to Mercury, Mr. Starr. I don't know what happened before then, but these last few months he's been under a great strain."

"Why?"

"He feels responsible for the accidents that have been interfering with the progress of Project Light."

"Is he responsible?"

"No, of course not. But you can see how he feels. He's sure everyone blames him. Project Light is vitally important. A great deal of money and effort has been put into it. Mindes is in charge of ten construction men, all five to ten years older than he is, and of an enormous amount of equipment."

"How does it happen he's so young?"

The doctor smiled grimly, but despite his grimness his white, even teeth made him look pleasant, even charming. He said, "Sub-etheric optics, Mr. Starr, is a completely new branch of science. Only young men, fresh out of school, know enough about it."

"You sound as though you know a bit about it yourself."

"Only what Mindes told me. We arrived in Mercury on the same ship, you know, and he fascinated me, quite won me over with what his project hopes to accomplish. Do you know about it?"

"Not a thing."

"Well, it involves hyperspace, that portion of space that lies outside the ordinary boundary of the space we know. The laws of nature that apply to ordinary space don't apply to hyperspace. For instance, in ordinary space it is impossible to move faster than the speed of light, so that it would take at least four years to reach the nearest star. In going through hyperspace any speed is possible——" The physician broke off with a sudden, apologetic smile. "You know all this, I'm sure."

"I suppose most people know that the discovery of hyperspatial flight made travel to the stars possible," said Lucky, "but what about Project Light?"

"Well," said Dr. Gardoma, "in ordinary space, light travels in straight lines in a vacuum. It can only be bent by large gravitational forces. In hyperspace, on the other hand, it can be bent as easily as if it were a cotton thread. It can be focused, dispersed, bent back upon itself. That's what the theory of hyperoptics says."

"And Scott Mindes, I suppose, is here to test that theory."

"That's right."

"Why here?" asked Lucky. "I mean, why on Mercury?"

"Because there's no other planetary surface in the Solar System where there is such a concentration of light over so large an area. The effects Mindes is looking for can be detected most easily here. It would be a hundred times as expensive to set up the project on Earth, and results would be a hundred times as uncertain. So Mindes tells me."

"Only now we're having these accidents."

Dr. Gardoma snorted. "They're no accidents. And, Mr. Starr, they have to be stopped. Do you know what the success of Project Light would mean?" He drove on, caught up in the vision. "Earth would no longer be the slave of the Sun. Space stations circling Earth could intercept sunlight, push it through hyperspace, and spread it evenly over the Earth. The desert heat and the polar cold would vanish. The seasons would be rearranged to our liking. We could control the weather by controlling the distribution of sunlight. We could have eternal sunlight where we wanted it; night of any length where we wanted it. Earth would be an air-conditioned paradise."

"It would take time, I imagine."

"A great deal of it, but this is the beginning. . . . Look, I may be out of order here, but aren't you the David Starr who cleared up the matter of the food poisonings on Mars?"

There was an edge to Lucky's voice as he answered, and his brows contracted slightly. "What makes you think so?"

Dr. Gardoma said, "I am a physician, after all. The poisonings seemed at first to be a disease epidemic, and I was much interested in it at the time. There were rumors about a young Councilman's having played the chief role in straightening the mystery, and names were mentioned."

Lucky said, "Suppose we let it go at that." He was displeased, as always, at any intimation that he was becoming well known. First Mindes, now Gardoma.

Dr. Gardoma said, "But if you are that Starr, you're here, I hope, to stop these so-called accidents."

Lucky did not seem to hear. He said, "When will I be able to talk to Scott Mindes, Dr. Gardoma?"

"Not for at least twelve hours."

"And will he be rational?"

"I'm certain of that."

A new guttural baritone voice broke in. "Are you, Gardoma? Is that because you know our boy Mindes was never irrational?"

Dr. Gardoma whirled at the sound and made no effort to hide the look of acute dislike on his face. "What are you doing here, Urteil?"

"Keeping my eyes and ears open, though I suppose you'd rather I kept them closed," the newcomer said.

Both Lucky and Bigman were staring at him curiously. He was a large man; not tall, but broad of shoulder and thick-muscled. His cheeks were blue with stubble, and there was a rather unpleasant air of self-assurance about him.

Dr. Gardoma said, "I don't care what you do with your eyes and ears, but not in my office, if you don't mind."

"Why not in your office?" demanded Urteil. "You're a doctor. Patients have a right to come in. Maybe I'm a patient."

"What's your complaint?"

"How about these two? What are their complaints? Hormone deficiency, for one thing, I suppose." His eyes fell lazily on Bigman Jones as he said that.

There was a breathless interlude in which Bigman turned a deathly white and then seemed to swell. Slowly he rose from his seat, his eyes round and staring. His lips moved as though forming the words "hormone deficiency," as though he were trying to convince himself that he had actually heard the words and that it was no illusion.

Then, with the speed of a cobra striking, Bigman's five foot two of cord-whip muscle launched itself at the broad, sneering figure before him.

But Lucky moved faster. His hands shot downward, catching Bigman at each shoulder. "Easy, Bigman."

The small Martian struggled desperately. "You heard him, Lucky. You heard him."

"Not now, Bigman."

Urteil's laugh was a series of sharp barks. "Let him go, fella. I'll smear the little boy over the floor with my finger."

Bigman howled and writhed in Lucky's grip.

Lucky said, "I wouldn't say anything else, Urteil, or

you may be in a kind of trouble your senator friend won't be able to get you out of."

His eyes had become brown ice as he spoke and his voice was smooth steel.

Urteil's glance locked with Lucky's for a moment, then fell away. He mumbled something about joking. Bigman's harsh breathing calmed somewhat, and as Lucky slowly released his grip the Martian took his seat, still trembling with almost unbearable fury.

Dr. Gardoma, who had watched the bit of byplay tensely, said, "You know Urteil, Mr. Starr?"

"By reputation. He's Jonathan Urteil, Senator Swenson's roving investigator."

"Well, call it that," muttered the physician.

"And I know you too, David Starr, Lucky Starr, whatever you call yourself," said Urteil. "You're the roving wonder-boy for the Council of Science. Mars poisonings. Asteroid pirates. Venusian telepathy. Do I have the list correct?"

"You have," said Lucky tonelessly.

Urteil grinned triumphantly. "There isn't much the senator's office doesn't know about the Council of Science. And there isn't much I don't know about things happening here. For instance, I know about the attempt on your life, and I've come here to see you about it."

"Why?"

"To give you a little warning. Just a friendly little warning. I suppose the medic here has been telling you what a nice guy Mindes is. Just a momentary splash of unbearable strain, he's been telling you, I suppose. They're great friends, Mindes and he."

"I just said——" began Dr. Gardoma.

"Let *me* say," said Urteil. "Let me say this. Scott Mindes is about as harmless as a two-ton asteroid heading for a space-ship. He wasn't temporarily insane when he pointed a blaster at you. He knew what he was doing. He tried to kill you in cold blood, Starr, and if you don't watch out, he'll succeed next time. Because you can bet your small friend's Martian hip boots he'll try again."

3

DEATH WAITS IN A ROOM

THE SILENCE THAT FOLLOWED SEEMED PLEASANT for no one but Urteil.

Then Lucky said, "Why? What's his motive?"

Urteil said calmly, "Because he's afraid. He's out here with millions of cash invested, cash that's been given him by a lax Council of Science, and he can't make his experiments work. He's calling his incompetence bad breaks. Eventually he'll go back to Earth and cry about Mercury's jinx. Then he'll get more money out of the Council, or, rather, out of the taxpayers, for some other fool scheme. Now you're coming to Mercury to investigate, and he's afraid that the Council, in spite of itself, may learn a little of the truth—— You take it from there."

Lucky said, "If this is the truth, you know it already."

"Yes, and I hope to prove it."

"But you're the danger to Mindes, then. By your reasoning, it is *you* he should try to kill."

Urteil grinned and his plump cheeks broadened until his jowly face looked wider than it was long. He said, "He *has* tried to kill me. True enough. But I've been through many tough sieges working for the senator. I can handle myself."

"Scott Mindes never tried to kill you or anybody," said Dr. Gardoma, his face pinched and white. "You know it, too."

27

Urteil made no direct answer. He spoke instead to Lucky. "And keep an eye on the good doctor too. As I said, he's great friends with Mindes. If I were you, I wouldn't let him treat me for as much as a headache. Pills and injections can——" He snapped his fingers with a sharp cracking noise.

Dr. Gardoma, words coming thickly, said, "Someday, someone will kill you for——"

Urteil said carelessly, "Yes? Are you planning on being the one?" He turned to go, then said over his shoulder, "Oh, I forgot. I hear that old man Peverale wants to see you. He's very disturbed at there being no official welcome. He's upset. So go see him and pat his poor old head for him—— And, Starr, another hint. After this, don't use any protective suits of any kind without checking them for leaks. Know what I mean?" With that, finally, he left.

Long moments passed before Gardoma was near normality again, before he could talk without choking. Then he said, "He riles me more every time I see him. He's a mean-mouthed, lying—"

"A mighty shrewd fellow," said Lucky dryly. "It seems obvious that one of his methods of attack is deliberately to say exactly what is calculated most to anger his opponent. An angry opponent is a half-helpless one. . . . And, Bigman, that goes for you. You can't just flail away at anyone who hints you're under six feet."

"Lucky," wailed the pint-sized Martian, "he said I was hormone-deficient."

"Then learn to wait for the appropriate moment to convince him otherwise."

Bigman grumbled rebelliously, and one clenched fist beat softly against the tough plastic of his silver-and-vermilion hip boots (the colorfully designed hip boots that no one but a Martian farm boy would wear and which no Martian farm boy would be without. Bigman owned a dozen, each more glaring than the last).

Lucky said, "Well, we'll look up Dr. Peverale. He's the head of the Observatory, isn't he?"

"The head of the whole Dome," said the doctor. "Actually, he's getting old and he's lost touch. I'm glad to say that he hates Urteil as much as any of us do, but there's nothing he can do about it. He can't buck the senator. I wonder if the Council of Science can?" he ended gloomily.

Lucky said, "I think so. Now remember, I'll want to see Mindes when he wakes up."

"All right. Take care of yourself."

Lucky stared at him curiously. "Take care of myself? How do you mean?"

Dr. Gardoma flushed. "Just an expression. I always say it. I don't mean anything by it."

"I see. Well, then, we'll be meeting again. Come along, Bigman, and stop frowning."

Dr. Lance Peverale shook them both by the hand with a vigor that was surprising in a man so old. His dark eyes were lit with concern and appeared the darker for the white eyebrows that topped them. His hair, still abundant, retained a considerable amount of its original color and had not faded past an iron gray. His lined and leathery cheeks, above which sharp cheekbones stood out prominently, did most to give him the appearance of age.

He spoke slowly and gently. "I am sorry, gentlemen, most concerned that you should have had such a distressing experience so soon after arriving at the Observatory. I blame myself."

"You have no reason to, Dr. Peverale," said Lucky.

"The fault is mine, sir. Had I been here to greet you as I ought to have—— But there, we were following an important and quite anomalous prominence, and I'm afraid I allowed my profession to tempt me from the proper expression of hospitality."

"In any case, you are forgiven," said Lucky, and he glanced sidewise with some amusement at Bigman, who was listening, open-mouthed, to the old man's stately flow of words.

"I am past forgiveness," said the astronomer, "but it

pleases me that you make the attempt. Meanwhile, I have ordered that quarters be placed at your disposal." He linked arms with both of them, urging them along the well-lit but narrow corridors of the Dome. "Our facilities are crowded, particularly since Dr. Mindes and his engineers have arrived and—and others. Still, I imagine you will find it welcome to have an opportunity to refresh yourselves and to sleep, perhaps. You will wish for food, I am sure, and it will be sent to you. Tomorrow will be time enough for you to meet us all socially, and for us to find out your purpose in coming here. For myself, the fact that the Council of Science vouches for you is sufficient. We will have a kind of banquet in your honor."

The corridor level was sinking as they walked, and they were burrowing into Mercury's vitals toward the residential level of the Dome.

Lucky said, "You are very kind. Perhaps I will also have the opportunity to inspect the Observatory."

Peverale seemed delighted at that. "I will be at your service in the matter, and I am sure you will not regret time spent in such an inspection. Our major equipment is mounted on a movable platform designed to move with the advancing or receding Terminator. In that fashion, a particular portion of the Sun can be kept continually in view despite Mercury's motions."

"Wonderful! But now, Dr. Peverale, one question. What is your opinion of Dr. Mindes? I'd appreciate a frank answer without any consideration for such things as diplomacy."

Peverale frowned. "Are you a sub-temporal engineer too?"

"Not quite," said Lucky, "but I was asking about Dr. Mindes."

"Exactly. Well"— and the astronomer looked thoughtful—"he is a pleasant young man, quite competent, I should think, but nervous, very nervous. He is easily offended, too easily offended. It has shown up as time has gone on and things have not been quite right with his project, and it is making him a little difficult to get along with. A pity, for as I say, he is a pleasant young man, otherwise. I am his superior, of course, while he is here at the Dome, but I don't really interfere with him. His project has no connection with our Observatory work."

"And your opinion of Jonathan Urteil?"

The old astronomer stopped walking on the instant. "What about him?"

"How does he get along here?"

"I am not interested in discussing the man," said Peverale.

They walked on in silence for a short while. The astronomer's face was lowering.

Lucky said, "Are there any other outsiders at the Dome? There are you and your men, Mindes and his men, and Urteil. Anyone else?"

"The doctor, of course. Dr. Gardoma."

"You do not consider him one of your own men?"

"Well, he's a doctor and not an astronomer. He supplies the one service the Dome must have and can't use machinery for. He cares for our health. He's new here."

"How new?"

"He replaced our old doctor after the latter's one-year shift. Dr. Gardoma arrived on the same ship that carried Mindes's group, as a matter of fact."

"One-year shift? Is that common for doctors here?"

"And most of the men. It makes it difficult to keep up continuity, and it is hard to train a man and have him leave; but then, Mercury is not an easy place to remain, and our men must be replaced frequently."

"Then in the last six months how many new men have you received here?"

"Perhaps twenty. The exact figures are in our records, but twenty is about it."

"Surely you yourself have been here quite a while."

The astronomer laughed. "Many years. I hate to think how many. And Dr. Cook, my assistant director, has been here for six years. Of course we take vacations frequently. . . . Well, here are your quarters, gentlemen. If there is anything you should wish, do not hesitate to inform me."

Bigman looked about him. The room was a small one, but it held two beds that could fold up into a wall recess when not in use; two chairs of which the same was true; a one-piece desk-chair combination; a small closet; and an adjoining wash room.

"Hey," he said, "a lot better than the ship, anyway, huh?"

"Not bad," said Lucky. "This is probably one of their better rooms."

"Why not?" said Bigman. "I guess he knows who *you* are."

"I guess not, Bigman," said Lucky. "He thought I might be a sub-temporal engineer. All he knows is that the Council sent me."

"Everyone else knows who you are," said Bigman.

"Not everyone. Mindes, Gardoma, and Urteil. . . . Look, Bigman, why don't you use the washroom? I'll have some food sent up and have them bring in the general utility kit from the *Shooting Starr*."

"Suits me," said Bigman cheerily.

Bigman sang loudly through the shower. As usual on a waterless world, the bath water was strictly rationed, with stern warnings on the wall as to the amount it was permissible to use. But Bigman had been born and bred on Mars. He had a huge respect for water and would no more think of splashing idly in it than in beef stew. So he used detergent copiously and water carefully and sang loudly.

He stepped in front of the forced-hot-air dryer which tingled his skin with its jets of bone-dry air and slapped his body with his hands to enhance the effect.

"Hey, Lucky," he yelled, "is there food on the table? I'm hungry."

He heard Lucky's voice speaking softly but could make out no words.

"Hey, Lucky," he repeated, and stepped out of the washroom. The desk had two steaming platters of roast beef and potatoes on it. (A slight sharpness in the aroma indicated the meat, at least, to be really a yeast imitation from the sub-sea gardens of Venus.) Lucky, however, was not eating, but sat on the bed and spoke into the room's Talkie.

Dr. Peverale's face was gazing out of the receiving plate.

Lucky said, "Well, then, was it general knowledge that this was to be our room?"

"Not general knowledge, but I gave the order to prepare your room over an open hookup. There was no reason for secrecy as far as I could see. I suppose anyone might have overheard. Furthermore, your room is one of a few such that are reserved for distinguished guests. There is no secret about it."

"I see. Thank you, sir."

"Is anything wrong?"

"Not at all," said Lucky, smiling, and broke connection. His smile disappeared and he looked thoughtful.

"Nothing wrong, my foot," exploded Bigman. "What's up, Lucky? Don't tell *me* there isn't anything wrong."

"Something is wrong, yes. I've been looking at the equipment here. These are special insulated suits for use on the Sun-side, I imagine."

Bigman lifted one of the suits hanging in a special wall recess. It was amazingly light for its bulk, nor could that be attributed to Mercurian gravity, since gravity here in the Dome was maintained at Earth-normal.

He shook his head. As usual, if he had to use a suit supplied him out of stock rather than one built to specifications, he would have to reduce all fittings to the minimum and even so find it inconvenient to use. He sighed resignedly. It was the penalty he paid for not being exactly tall. He always thought of it that way: "not exactly tall." He never thought of his five foot two as being actually "short."

He said, "Sands of Mars, they've got everything here for us, all set and waiting. Bed. Bath. Food. Suits."

"And something else too," said Lucky gravely. "Death is waiting in this room. See here."

Lucky lifted one arm of the larger suit. The ball joint at the shoulder moved easily, but where it joined the shaft of the shoulder there was a tiny, all but unnoticeable gap. It would have been completely unnoticeable if Lucky's fingers had not spread it apart.

It was a slash! Man-made, obviously! Insulation showed.

"On the inner surface," said Lucky, "There's a similar slash. This suit would have lasted just long enough to get me out on the Sun-side, and then it would have killed me neatly."

4

OVER THE BANQUET TABLE

"Urteil!" cried Bigman at once, with a ferocity that stiffened every muscle of his small body. "That dirty cobber——"

"Why Urteil?" asked Lucky softly.

"He warned us to watch our suits, Lucky. Remember?"

"Of course. And it's exactly what I did."

"Sure. He set it up for us. We find a slashed suit and we think he's a great guy. Then we're cold meat for him next time around. Don't fall for that, Lucky. He's a——"

"Now wait, Bigman, wait! Don't make your mind up so fast. Look at it this way. Urteil said Mindes had tried to kill him, too. Suppose we believe him. Suppose Mindes had tried to gimmick Urteil's suit and Urteil had spotted it in time. Urteil would warn us to watch out for the same trick. Maybe Mindes did this."

"Sands of Mars, Lucky, that can't be. This guy, Mindes, is ladled full of sleeping pills, and before that he wasn't out of our sight from the minute we got onto this miserable rock."

"All right. How do we know Mindes is asleep and under medication?" asked Lucky.

"Gardoma says——" began Bigman, and fell silent.

"Exactly. Gardoma says! We haven't seen Mindes, though. We only know what Dr. Gardoma said, and Dr. Gardoma is a great friend of Mindes's."

"The two of them are in it together," said Bigman, with instant conviction. "Jumping comets——"

"Wait, wait, don't *you* jump so. Great Galaxy, Bigman, I'm just trying to straighten out my thoughts, and you take me up on everything." His tone was as disapproving as it could ever be with respect to his small friend. He went on, "Now you've complained a dozen times that I don't tell you everything on my mind until everything's done with. This is why, you blaster-happy nitwit. As soon as I advance a theory, you're off on a charge, all your weapons cocked and ready."

"I'm sorry, Lucky," said Bigman. "Go ahead."

"All right. Now Urteil is easy to suspect. Nobody likes him. Even Dr. Peverale doesn't. You saw how he reacted just to the mention of his name. We've met him only once and you dislike him——"

"I'll say," muttered Bigman.

"——while I don't exactly like him, either. Anyone can slash this suit and hope that suspicion will fall on Urteil if it should happen to be discovered, and it would be surely discovered after it's killed someone, if not before."

"I see all that, Lucky."

"On the other hand," went on Lucky smoothly, "Mindes has already tried to get rid of me with a blaster. If that were a serious attempt, he doesn't seem the type to do anything as indirect as suit-slashing. As for Dr. Gardoma, I don't see him involving himself in the murder of a Councilman just out of friendship for Mindes."

"Then what's the decision?" cried Bigman impatiently.

"There isn't any so far," said Lucky, "except maybe that we go to sleep." He turned down the bed sheets and stepped into the washroom.

Bigman looked after him and shrugged his shoulders.

Scott Mindes was sitting up in bed when Lucky and

Bigman entered his quarters the next morning. He was pale and looked tired.

"Hello," he said. "Karl Gardoma told me what happened. You don't know how sorry I am."

Lucky passed it off with a shrug. "How do you feel?"

"Wrung out but all right, if you know what I mean. I'll be at the dinner party old Peverale is giving tonight."

"Is that wise?"

"I won't leave Urteil there holding the fort," said Mindes, hatred suddenly flooding his face with momentary color, "telling everyone I'm crazy. Or Dr. Peverale, either, for that matter."

"Dr. Peverale doubts your sanity?" asked Lucky softly.

"Well—— Look, Starr, I've been scouting the Sunside in a small rocket-scooter ever since the accidents started getting bad. I had to do it. It's my project. Twice, now, I—I've seen something."

Mindes paused and Lucky prodded him. "Seen what, Dr. Mindes?"

"I wish I could say for sure. I saw it only from a distance each time. Something moving. Something that looked human. Something in a space-suit. Not one of our inso-suits, our special insulated jobs, you know. It looked more like an ordinary space-suit. Ordinary metal, you know."

"Did you try to get closer?"

"Yes, and I lost it. And the photographs showed nothing either. Just spots of light and dark that might have been something, or nothing. But it was something, all right. Something that moved under the Sun as though it didn't care a thing for the heat and radiation. It would even stand still in the Sun for minutes at a time. That's what got me."

"Is that strange? Standing still, I mean?"

Mindes laughed shortly. "On the Mercury Sun-side? It sure is. Nobody stands still. Insulated suit and all, you go about your business as fast as you can and get out from under as fast as you can. This near the Terminator the heat isn't so bad. It's the radiation, though. It's just good practice to take as little of it as possible. The inso-suits aren't complete protection against gamma rays. If you must stand still, you move into the shade of a rock."

"What's your explanation of it all?"

Mindes's voice fell to an almost shamed whisper. "I don't think it's a man."

"You're not going to say it's a two-legged ghost, are you?" said Bigman suddenly, before Lucky could nudge him into silence.

But Mindes only shook his head. "Did I use that phrase on the surface? I seem to remember—— No, I think it's a Mercurian."

"What?" cried Bigman, sounding as if he thought that were worse.

"How else could it endure the Sun's radiation and heat so?"

"Why would it need a space-suit then?" asked Lucky.

"Well, I don't know." Mindes's eyes flashed, and a restless wildness settled upon them. "But it's *something*. When I got back to the Dome, every man and every suit could be accounted for each time. Dr. Peverale won't authorize an expedition to make a real search. He says we're not equipped for it."

"Have you told him what you told me?"

"He thinks I'm crazy. I'm sure of it. He thinks I'm seeing reflections and building men out of them in my imagination. But that's not so, Starr!"

Lucky said, "Have you contacted the Council of Science?"

"How can I? Dr. Peverale wouldn't back me. Urteil would say I was mad and they would listen to *him*. Who would listen to me?"

"I would," said Lucky.

Mindes sat up in bed with a jerk. His hand shot out as though it were ready to grasp the other's sleeve but then held back. He said, in a choked voice, "Then you'll investigate it?"

"In my way," promised Lucky, "I will."

The others were already at the banquet table that evening when Lucky and Bigman arrived. Above the hum of greeting that rose as they entered and the beginning of the introductions, there were obvious signs that the gathering was not entirely a pleasant one.

Dr. Peverale sat at the head of the table, his thin lips set and his sunken cheeks quivering, the picture of dignity maintained under difficulty. At his left was the broad-shouldered figure of Urteil, lounging back in his chair, thick fingers playing delicately with the rim of a drinking glass.

Toward the foot of the table was Scott Mindes, looking painfully young and tired as he stared with angry frustration at Urteil. Next to him was Dr. Gardoma, watching with an anxious and thoughtful eye as though ready to interfere in case Mindes grew rash.

The remaining seats, except for two empty ones at Dr. Peverale's right, were occupied by several of the senior men of the Observatory. One in particular, Hanley Cook, second in command at the Dome, leaned his tall, lean body forward and took Lucky's hand firmly in his own.

Lucky and Bigman took their seats and the salads were served.

Urteil said at once in a harsh voice that effectively took over the conversation, "We were wondering just before you came in whether young Mindes ought not to tell you of the great wonders in store for Earth as a result of his experiments."

"No such thing," snapped Mindes, "and I'll do my own talking if you don't mind."

"Oh, come on, Scott," said Urteil, grinning broadly, "don't be bashful. Well, then, look here, *I'll* tell the man."

Dr. Gardoma's hand fell, as though by accident, on

Mindes's shoulder, and the young engineer swallowed a cry of indignation and remained silent.

Urteil said, "Now I warn you, Starr, this is going to be good. It——"

Lucky interrupted, "I know something of the experiments. The grand result of an air-conditioned planet is quite possible, I think."

Urteil scowled. "That so? I'm glad you're optimistic. Poor Scott can't even make the pilot experiment work. Or at least he says he can't, don't you, Scott?"

Mindes half rose, but again Dr. Gardoma's hand was on his shoulder.

Bigman's eyes traveled from speaker to speaker, resting on Urteil with black distaste. He said nothing.

The arrival of the main course stopped the conversation momentarily, and Dr. Peverale tried desperately to turn it into less explosive channels. For a while he succeeded, but then Urteil, with the last of his helping of roast beef impaled on his fork, leaned toward Lucky and said, "So you go for the project Mindes is running, do you?"

"I think it's a reasonable one."

"You have to think that, being a member of the Council of Science. But what if I told you that the experiments here were phony; they could be run on Earth for one per cent of the cost if the Council were only interested enough in the taxpayers' money to save a little of it. What would you say if I told you that?"

"The same I would say if you told me anything at all," retorted Lucky composedly. "I would say, Mr. Urteil, that the chances are that you're lying. It's your greatest talent and, I believe, pleasure."

Instantly a great silence fell on the banqueters, even on Urteil. His thick cheeks seemed to sag in surprise and his eyes to bulge. With sudden passion, he leaned directly across Dr. Peverale's place, rising from his seat and bringing his right hand down hard and flat just short of Lucky's platter.

"No Council lackey——" he began in a roar.

And as he did that, Bigman moved, too. No eye at

the table saw the details of that move, since it flashed with the speed of a striking snake, but Urteil's roar ended in a shout of dismay.

Urteil's hand, which had come down with such hard finality, now showed the carved metallic haft of a force-knife growing out of it.

Dr. Peverale scraped his chair back suddenly, and there was a cry or an exclamation from every man there but Bigman himself. Even Lucky seemed startled.

Bigman's tenor voice rose in delight. "Spread your fingers, you tub of mineral oil. Spread them and then grease back down into your seat."

Urteil stared at his small tormenter without understanding for a moment and then very slowly spread his fingers. His hand was not hurt, not a sliver of skin had been removed. The force-knife stood quivering in the hard plastic table top, an inch of its waveringly luminescent force-blade (it wasn't matter, merely a thin field of immaterial force) in sight. The knife had entered the table, working its way neatly and unerringly between the second and third finger of Urteil's hand.

Urteil snatched his hand away as though it were suddenly in flames.

Bigman crowed with delight and said, "And next time you reach a hand in Lucky's direction or in mine, you cobber, I chop it right off. What would you say if I told you that? And whatever you say, say it politely." He reached out for the force-knife, deactivating the blade as he seized the haft, and returned it to its inconspicuous holster on his belt.

Lucky said, with a light frown, "I wasn't aware that my friend was armed. I'm sure he's sorry for having disturbed the meal, but I believe Mr. Urteil may take this incident to heart."

Someone laughed and there was a tight smile on Mindes's face.

Urteil looked with hot eyes from face to face. He said, "I won't forget this treatment. It's obvious to me that the senator is receiving little co-operation, and he'll hear of that. And meanwhile, I'm staying right here."

He folded his arms as though daring anyone to make him leave.

Little by little the conversation grew general.

Lucky said to Dr. Peverale, "You know, sir, it seems to me that your face is familiar."

"Is it?" The astronomer smiled in a strained fashion. "I don't think I ever met you before."

"Well, were you ever on Ceres?"

"Ceres?" The old astronomer looked at Lucky with some surprise. He had obviously not yet recovered from the force-knife episode. "The largest observatory in the Solar System is on that asteroid. I worked there as a young man, and I frequently visit it even now."

"Then I wonder if I didn't perhaps see you there."

Lucky couldn't help thinking, as he spoke, of those exciting days when the chase was on for Captain Anton and the pirates who were making their lair in the asteroids. And particularly the day when the pirate ships raided the very heart of Council territory, onto the surface of Ceres itself, winning out temporarily by the very daring of their undertaking.

But Dr. Peverale was shaking his head in gentle good humor. "I would have been certain, sir, had I had the pleasure of seeing you there. I am sure I did not."

"Too bad," said Lucky.

"The loss is mine, I assure you. But then it was my season for loss. As a result of an intestinal ailment, I missed all the excitement in connection with the pirate raid. I knew of it only through the conversations I overheard among my nurses."

Dr. Peverale looked about the table now, his good humor restored. The dessert was being served by the mechanical tray-carrier. He said, "Gentlemen, there has been some discussion of Project Light."

He paused to smile benignly, then went on. "It isn't exactly a happy subject under the circumstances, but I have been thinking a good deal about the accidents that have disturbed so many of us. It seems it would be a good time for me to give you all my thoughts on the matter. After all, Dr. Mindes is here. We have had a good meal. And, finally, I have something interesting to say."

Urteil broke a long silence to ask grimly, *"You,* Dr. Peverale?"

The astronomer said mildly, "Why not? I have had interesting things to say many times in my life. And I *will* say what's on my mind now." There was a sudden gravity about him. "I believe I know the whole truth, the exact truth. I know who is causing the destruction in connection with Project Light and why."

5

THE DIRECTION OF DANGER

THE OLD ASTRONOMER'S GENTLE FACE seemed pleased
as he looked about the table, perhaps at having gained
so absolutely the attention of all. Lucky looked about
the table too. He caught the expressions that greeted
Dr. Peverale's statement. There was contempt on Urteil's broad features, a puzzled frown on Dr. Gardoma's
face, a sulkier one on that of Mindes. The others were
held in various attitudes of curiosity and interest.

One man caught Lucky's attention particularly. It
was Hanley Cook, Dr. Peverale's second in command.
He stared at his finger ends, and there was something
like weary disgust about him. When he looked up, his
expression had changed and settled into a cautious
blankness.

Nevertheless Lucky thought: I'll have to talk to the
man.

And then his attention shifted back to Dr. Peverale.

Dr. Peverale was saying, "The saboteur can't be one
of us, of course. Dr. Mindes tells me that he has
investigated and is sure of that. Even without investigation, I am sure that none of us is capable of such
criminal action. Yet the saboteur must be intelligent,
since the destruction is too purposeful, too exclusively
directed against Project Light, to be the result of
chance or of anything nonintelligent. Therefore——"

Bigman interrupted excitedly. "Hey, you mean
Mercury has native life? It's Mercurians doing this?"

There was a sudden buzz of confused comment and some laughter, at which Bigman reddened. "Well," said the small Martian, "isn't that what Dr. Peverale is saying?"

"Not quite," said Dr. Peverale gently.

"There is no life of any kind native to Mercury," said one of the astronomers with emphasis. "That's one thing we're sure of."

Lucky interposed, "How sure? Has anyone looked?"

The astronomer who had spoken seemed taken aback. He said, "There have been exploring parties. Certainly."

Lucky smiled. He had met intelligent beings on Mars that no other man knew of. He had discovered semi-intelligent beings on Venus where none had been thought to exist. He, for one, was not ready to admit that any planet lacked life, or even intelligence.

He said, "How many exploring parties? How thorough was each exploration? Has every square mile been searched?"

The astronomer did not answer. He looked away, raising his eyebrows as though to say: What's the use?

Bigman grinned, his little face wrinkling into a caricature of gnomish good humor.

Dr. Peverale said, "My dear Starr, explorations have uncovered nothing. While we grant that the possibility of Mercurian life is not completely excluded, the probability of its existence is very low. Suppose we assume that the only intelligent life in the Galaxy is the human race. Certainly, it's the only one we know of."

With the Martian mind-beings in his memory, Lucky did not agree with that, but he kept silent and let the old man continue.

It was Urteil, little by little having recovered his self-possession, who intervened. "What do you think you're getting at," he asked, and it was characteristic of the man that he could not resist adding, "if anything?"

Dr. Peverale did not answer Urteil directly. He looked from face to face, deliberately ignoring the Congressional investigator. He said, "The point is, there are humans elsewhere than on Earth. There are humans in many star systems." A queer change came across the astronomer's face. It pinched in, grew white, and his nostrils flared as though he were suddenly overpowered with anger. "For instance, there are humans on the planets of Sirius. What if they are the saboteurs?"

"Why should they be?" asked Lucky at once.

"Why not? They have committed aggression against Earth before."

So much was true. Lucky Starr himself had helped, not too long before, to repel a Sirian invasion flotilla that had landed on Ganymede, but in that case they had left the Solar System without pushing matters to a showdown. Yet, on the other hand, it was a common thing for many Earthmen to blame Sirians for anything that went wrong.

Dr. Peverale was saying with energy, "I've *been* there. I've *been* to Sirius only five months ago. It took a great deal of red tape because Sirius welcomes neither immigrants nor visitors, but it was a matter of an interstellar astronomical convention, and I managed to get a visa. I was determined to see for myself, and I must say I wasn't disappointed.

"The planets of Sirius are thinly populated and they are extremely decentralized. They live in isolated individual family units, each with its own energy source and services. Each has its group of mechanical slaves— there's no other word possible—slaves in the shape of positronic robots, which do the labor. The Sirian humans maintain themselves as a fighting aristocracy. Every one of them can handle a space-cruiser. They'll never rest till they destroy the Earth."

Bigman shifted restlessly in his seat. "Sands of Mars, let them try. Let them try, is all I say."

"They will when they are quite ready," said Dr. Peverale, "and, unless we do something quickly to meet the danger, they will win. What have we got to oppose them? A population in the billions, true, but how many can handle themselves in space? We are six billion rabbits and they are one million wolves. Earth is helpless and grows more helpless every year. We are fed by grain from Mars and yeast from Venus. We get our minerals from the asteroids, and we used to get them from Mercury, too, when the mines here were working.

"Why, Starr, if Project Light succeeds, Earth will be dependent on space stations for the manner in which it gets its very sunshine. Don't you see how vulnerable that makes us? A Sirian raiding party, by attacking the outposts of the System, could panic and starve Earth without ever having to fight us directly.

"And can we do anything to them in return? No matter how many of them we kill, the remaining Sirians are always self-contained and self-sufficient. Any of them could continue the war."

The old man was almost breathless with passion. There was no questioning his sincerity. It was as though he were getting something out of himself that had been stifling him.

Lucky's eye wandered back to Dr. Peverale's second, Hanley Cook. The man was resting his forehead on the bony knuckles of one large hand. His face was flushed, but to Lucky it did not seem like a flush of either anger or indignation. Rather, it seemed one of embarrassment.

Scott Mindes spoke up skeptically. "What would be the point, Dr. Peverale? If they're getting along on Sirius, why should they come to Earth? What would they get out of us? Even supposing they conquer Earth, they would only have to support us——"

"Nonsense!" rapped out the senior astronomer. "Why should they? They would want Earth's resources, not Earth's population. Get that through your head. They'd let us starve. It would be part of their policy."

"Oh, come," said Gardoma. "That's unbelievable."

"Not out of cruelty," said Dr. Peverale, "out of policy. They despise us. They consider us scarcely more than animals. The Sirians themselves are very race-conscious. Since Earthmen first colonized Sirius, they have been breeding themselves carefully until they are free of diseases and of various characteristics which they consider undesirable.

"They are of uniform appearance, while Earthmen are of all shapes, sizes, colors, varieties. The Sirians consider us inferior. That's why they won't let us emigrate to Sirius. They wouldn't let me attend the convention till the government pulled every string possible. Astronomers from other systems were all welcome but not from Earth.

"And human life, any kind of human life, doesn't mean much to them, anyway. They're machine-centered. I've watched them with their metal men. They're more considerate of a Sirian robot, almost, than of a Sirian man. They would regard a robot as worth a hundred men of Earth. They pamper those robots. They love them. Nothing's too good for them."

Lucky murmured, "Robots are expensive. They have to be treated carefully."

Maybe so," said Dr. Peverale, "but men who become accustomed to worrying about the needs of machines become callous about the needs of men."

Lucky Starr leaned forward, elbows on the table, dark eyes serious and the smooth vertical lines of his handsome, still subtly boyish face set gravely. He said, "Dr. Peverale, if the Sirians are race-conscious and are breeding themselves into uniformity, they will defeat themselves in the long run. It is variety in the human race that brings about progress. It is Earth and not Sirius that is in the forefront of scientific research. Earthmen settled Sirius in the first place, and it is we, not our Sirian cousins, who are advancing in new directions every year. Even the positronic robots you mention were invented and developed on Earth by Earthmen."

"Yes," said the astronomer, "but Earthmen don't make use of the robot. It would upset our economy, and we place the comfort and security of today above the safety of tomorrow. We use our scientific advance to make ourselves weaker. Sirius uses its to make itself stronger. That's the difference and that's the danger."

Dr. Peverale threw himself back in his chair, looking grim. The mechanical tray-carrier cleared the table.

Lucky pointed at it. "That's a sort of a robot, if you like," he said.

The mechanical tray-carrier went quietly about its task. It was a flat-surfaced thing moving smoothly on a diamagnetic field, so that its gently curved base never actually touched the floor. Its limber tentacles removed dishes with careful delicacy, placing some on its upper surface, others within a cabinet in its side.

"That's a simple automaton," snorted Dr. Peverale. "It has no positronic brain. It cannot adapt itself to any change in its task."

"Well, then," said Lucky, "are you saying that the Sirians are sabotaging Project Light?"

"Yes. I am."

"Why should they?"

Dr. Peverale shrugged. "Perhaps it's just part of a larger plan. I don't know what trouble there is elsewhere in the Solar System. These may be the first random probings to prepare for ultimate invasion and conquest. Project Light in itself means nothing, the Sirian danger everything. I wish I could rouse the Council of Science and the government and the people to that truth."

Hanley Cook coughed, then spoke for the first time. "The Sirians are human like the rest of us. If they're on the planet, *where* are they?"

Dr. Peverale said coldly, "That's for an exploring expedition to find out. A well-prepared, well-equipped expedition."

"Wait a minute," said Mindes, his eyes glinting with excitement, "I've been out on the Sun-side, and I'll swear——"

"A well-prepared, well-equipped expedition," repeated the old astronomer firmly. "Your one-man flights mean nothing, Mindes."

The engineer stuttered a moment and slumped into an embarrassed silence.

Lucky said suddenly, "You seem to be unhappy

about this, Urteil. What is your opinion of Dr. Peverale's view?"

The investigator lifted his eyes and met those of
Lucky for a long moment in hatred and open defiance.
It was obvious he had not forgotten, nor would forget,
the earlier exchange at this table.

He said, "I'm keeping my opinion to myself. But I
will say this, I'm not fooled by anything that's going on
here tonight."

His mouth clamped shut and Lucky, having waited a
moment for further remarks, turned to Peverale and
said, "I wonder if we do need a complete expedition,
sir. If we suppose that the Sirians are here on Mercury,
can we perhaps deduce where they might be?"

"Go ahead, Lucky," crowed Bigman at once. "Show
them how."

Dr. Peverale said, "How do you mean?"

"Well, what would be the best for the Sirians? If
they've been sabotaging Project Light at frequent intervals over a period of months, it would be most conve-
nient for them to have a base near the project. Yet at
the same time, the base must not be easily detected.
They've certainly been successful in the second require-
ment, anyway. Now where could such a handy, but
secret, base be?

"Let's divide up Mercury into two parts, Sun-side
and dark-side. It seems to me that they would be
foolish to set up a base on Sun-side. Too hot, too much
radiation, too inhospitable."

Cook grunted. "No more inhospitable than the dark-
side."

"No, no," said Lucky at once, "you're wrong there.
The Sun-side presents an environment which is quite
unusual. Humans aren't accustomed to it at all. The
dark-side is something very familiar. It is simply
ground which is exposed to space, and the conditions of
space are very familiar. The dark-side is cold but no
colder than space. It is dark and airless but no darker
than any portion of space not in direct sunlight and
certainly no more airless. Men have learned to live

comfortably in space, and they can live on the dark-side."

"Go on," said Dr. Peverale, his old eyes gleaming with interest. "Go on, Mr. Starr."

"But establishing a base that would serve over a period of months is not a simple thing. They must have a ship or ships to get back to Sirius someday. Or if they're to be picked up by a ship from outside they must still have ample stores of food and water, as well as an energy source. All this takes up room, and yet they must be certain they will not be detected. It leaves only one place where they can be."

"Where, Lucky?" asked Bigman, nearly jumping up and down in his eagerness. He, at least, had no doubts that whatever Lucky said was so. "Where?"

"Well," said Lucky, "when I first arrived here, Dr. Mindes made mention of mines on Mercury which had failed. Just a few moments ago, Dr. Peverale spoke of mines on Mercury that were once working. From that I gather that there must be empty mine shafts and cor-ridors on the planet, and they must be either here or at the South Pole, since the polar regions are the only places where the temperature extremes are not too great. Am I right?"

Cook faltered. "Yes, there are mines here. Before the Observatory was established, the Dome was the mining center."

"Then we're sitting on top of a large empty hole in Mercury. If the Sirians are successfully hiding a large base, where else would it be? *There* is the direction of danger."

A murmur of appreciation passed around the table, but it was shattered abruptly by Urteil's guttural tones.

"All very pretty," he said, "but what does it all come to? What are you going to do about it?"

"Bigman and I," said Lucky, "intend to enter the mines just as soon as we can get ready. If there's anything there, we'll find it."

6

PREPARATIONS

Dr. Gardoma said sharply, "Do you intend to go alone?"

"Why not?" interposed Urteil. "The heroics are cheap enough. Of course they'll go alone. There's nothing and nobody there, and they know it."

"Care to join us?" asked Bigman. "If you leave your big mouth behind you can fit into a suit."

"You wouldn't crowd one even with yours," snarled Urteil.

Dr. Gardoma said again, "There's no point in going alone if——"

"A preliminary investigation," said Lucky, "will do no harm. Actually, Urteil may be right. There may be no one there. At the worst, we'll keep in touch with you at the Dome and hope that we can handle any Sirians we meet. Bigman and I are used to handling tight situations."

"Besides which," added Bigman, his gnomish face puckering into a grin, "Lucky and I like tight situations."

Lucky smiled and rose to his feet. "If we may be excused——"

Urteil at once rose, turned, and stamped away. Lucky's eyes followed him thoughtfully.

Lucky stopped Hanley Cook as the latter passed him. He touched his elbow gently.

Cook looked up, his eyes all concern. "Yes. What is it, sir?"

Lucky said quietly, "May I see you in our quarters as soon as possible?"

"I'll be there in fifteen minutes. Is that all right?"

"Fine."

Cook was very little later than that. He stepped into their quarters softly, wearing the look of concern that seemed a constant part of him. He was a man in his late forties with an angular face and light brown hair that was beginning to be touched with gray.

Lucky said, "I had forgotten to tell you where our quarters were. I'm sorry."

Cook looked surprised. "I knew where you were assigned."

"Well, good. Thank you for coming at our request."

"Oh," Cook paused. Then he said hurriedly, "Glad to. Glad to."

Lucky said, "There's a small matter of the insulation suits in this room. The ones intended for use on the Sun-side."

"The inso-suits? We didn't forget the instruction film, did we?"

"No, no. I viewed that. It's quite another thing."

Cook said, "Something wrong?"

"Something wrong?" crowed Bigman. "Look for yourself." He spread the arms in order to display the slashes.

Cook looked blank, then flushed slowly and grew round-eyed with horror. "I don't see—— It's impossible—— Here at the Dome!"

Lucky said, "The main thing is to get it replaced."

"But who would do such a thing? We must find out."

"No use disturbing Dr. Peverale."

"No, no," said Cook, at once, as though he had not thought of it before.

"We'll find out the details in due time. Meanwhile I would like to get it replaced."

"Certainly. I'll attend to it promptly. No wonder you

wanted to see me. Great Space——" He got to his feet
in a kind of speechlessness and made as though to go.

But Lucky stopped him. "Wait, this is a minor thing.
There are other things we must discuss. By the way,
before we get to that—I take it you did not agree with
Dr. Peverale's views on the Sirians."

Cook frowned. "I'd rather not discuss that."

"I watched you as he was speaking. You disap-
proved, I think."

Cook sat down again. His bony fingers clutched one
another in a tight clasp and he said, "He's an old man.
He's been all mixed up about the Sirians for years.
Psychopathic, almost. He sees them under his bed. He
blames them for everything. If our plates are overex-
posed, he blames them. Since he's been back from
Sirius he's worse than ever, because of what he claims
he went through."

"What was it he went through?"

"Nothing terrible, I suppose. But they quarantined
him. They assigned him a separate building. They were
too polite sometimes. They were too rude other times.
There was no way of suiting him, I suppose. Then they
forced a positronic robot on him to take care of personal services."

"Did he object to that too?"

"He claims it was because they wouldn't come near
him themselves. That's what I mean. He took *everything* as an insult."

"Were you with him?"

Cook shook his head. "Sirius would only accept one
man, and he's senior. I ought to have gone. He's too
old, really—too old."

Cook was talking in a brooding sort of way. He
looked up suddenly. "This is all confidential, by the
way."

"Completely," Lucky assured him.

"What about your friend?" said Cook uncertainly. "I
mean, I know he's honorable, but he's a little, uh,
hotheaded."

"Hey," began Bigman, stiffening.

Lucky's affectionate hand came down on the little
fellow's head and brushed his hair down on his forehead. "He's hotheaded, all right," he said, "as you saw
at the banquet table. I can't always stop him in time
and sometimes, when he's riled, he uses his tongue and
his fist instead of his head. That's something I always
have to keep in mind. Still, when I ask him specifically
to keep quiet about something, he is quiet, and that's
all there is to it."

"Thank you," said Cook.

Lucky went on. "To get back to my original question:
Do you agree with Dr. Peverale concerning the Sirians
in this present case?"

"I don't. How would they know about Project Light,
and why should they care? I don't see them sending
ships and men and risking trouble with the Solar System just so they can break a few cables. Of course, I
tell you this, Dr. Peverale has been feeling hurt for
quite a while now———"

"In what way?"

"Well, Mindes and his group were established here
while he was at Sirius. He came back and found them
here. He knew they were coming eventually. It's been
planned for years. Still, coming back and actually
finding them here was a shock."

"Has he tried to get rid of Mindes?"

"Oh no, nothing like that. He's even been friendly.
It's just that it makes him feel that someday he'll be
replaced altogether, maybe someday soon, and I suppose he hates the thought. So it's pleasant for him to
take charge and start a big affair about Sirians. That's
his baby, you see."

Lucky nodded, then said, "Tell me, have you ever
been on Ceres?"

Cook looked surprised at the change in subject but
said, "Occasionally. Why?"

"With Dr. Peverale? Alone?"

"With him, usually. He goes more frequently than I
do."

Lucky grinned. "Were you there at the time the pirates made their raid on Ceres last year?"

Cook smiled too. "No, but the old man was. We've heard the story several times. He was very angry about it. He's practically never sick, and this one time he was just completely out. He missed everything."

"Well, that's the way it goes. ... And, now, I think we'd better get to the main business. I didn't like to bother Dr. Peverale. As you say, he's an old man. You're his second and quite a bit younger——" Lucky smiled.

"Yes, of course. What can I do?"

"It's about the mines. I assume that somewhere at the Dome there are records, maps, charts, something which will tell us the arrangements of the main shafts and so on. Obviously, we can't wander at random."

"I'm sure there are," agreed Cook.

"And you can get them and perhaps go over them with us?"

"Yes, of course."

"Now as far as you know, Dr. Cook, the mines are in good shape, I hope. I mean, there's no danger of collapse or anything like that?"

"Oh no, I'm sure there's nothing of the sort possible. We're built right over some of the shafts, and we had to look into the engineering when the Observatory was first being set up. The shafts are well-buttressed and completely safe, particularly in Mercury's gravity."

"How come," asked Bigman, "the mines were shut down, if they're in such good shape?"

"A good question," said Cook, and a small smile broke through his expression of settled melancholy. "Do you want the true explanation or the interesting one?"

"Both," said Bigman at once.

Cook offered smokes to the others which were refused, then lit a cigarette after tamping it on the back of one hand in an abstracted manner. "The truth is this. Mercury is quite dense, and there were hopes that it would be a rich source of the heavy metals: lead, silver, mercury, platinum. It was, too; not as rich as might be, perhaps, but rich enough. Unfortunately, it was uneconomic. Supporting the mines here and transporting the ore back to Earth or even the Moon for processing raised the price too high.

"As for the interesting explanation, that's another thing completely. When the Observatory was first set up fifty years ago, the mines were still a going concern, though they were already closing down some of the shafts. The original astronomers heard stories from the miners and passed it on to the newcomers. It's part of the Mercurian legendry."

"What are the stories?" asked Bigman.

"It seems miners died in the shafts."

"Sands of Mars!" cried Bigman testily. "They die anywhere. You think anybody lives forever?"

"These were frozen to death."

"So?"

"It was a mysterious freezing. The shafts were fairly well heated in those days, and their suit power units were in operation. The stories accumulate embroidery, you know, and, eventually miners wouldn't go into the main shafts in anything but gangs, wouldn't go into the side shafts at all, and the mines shut down."

Lucky nodded. He said, "You'll get the plans for the mines?"

"Right off. And replacements for that inso-suit too."

Preparations proceeded as though for a major expedition. A new inso-suit, replacing the one that had been slashed, was brought and tested, then laid to one side. After all, it would be ordinary space-suits for the dark-side.

The charts were brought and studied. Together with Cook, Lucky sketched out a possible route of exploration, following the main shafts.

Lucky left Bigman to take care of packing the adjunct-units with homogenized food and with water (which could be swallowed while still in the suit), make sure of the charge of the power units and the pressure

on the oxygen tanks, inspect the working efficiency of
the waste disposal unit and the moisture recirculator.

He himself made a short trip to their ship, the *Shooting Starr*. He made the trip via the surface, carrying a
field pack, the contents of which he did not discuss with
Bigman. He returned without it but carrying two small
objects that looked like thick belt buckles, slightly
curved, in dull-steel finish and centered by a rectangle
in glassy red.

"What's that?" asked Bigman.

"Microergometers," said Lucky. "Experimental. You
know, like the ergometers on board ship except that
those are bolted to the floor."

"What can these things detect?"

"Nothing at a couple of hundred thousand miles like
a ship's ergometer, but it can detect atomic power
sources at ten miles, maybe. Look, Bigman, you ac-
tivate it here. See?"

Lucky's thumbnail exerted pressure against a small
slit in one side of the mechanism. A sliver of metal
moved in, then out, and instantly the red patch on the
surface glowed brightly. Lucky turned the small ergometer in this direction and that. In one particular position, the red patch glowed with the energy of a nova.

"That," said Lucky, "is probably the direction of the
Dome's power plant. We can adjust the mechanism to
zero that out. It's a little tricky." He worked painstak-
ingly on the adjustment of two small controls so
smoothly inset as nearly to be invisible.

He smiled as he worked, his engagingly youthful face
lighting with pleasure. "You know, Bigman, there isn't
a time I visit Uncle Hector but that he doesn't load me
up with the Council's latest gadgets. He claims that
with the chances you and I are always taking (you
know the way he talks) we need them. Sometimes,
though, I think he just wants us to act as field-testers
for the gadgets. This one, though, may be useful."

"How, Lucky?"

"For one thing, Bigman, if there are Sirians in the
mines, they'll have a small atomic power plant. They'll

have to. They'll need power for heat, for electrolyzing water, and so on. This ergometer should detect that at ample distance. And for another thing——"

He fell silent, and Bigman's lips compressed in chagrin. He knew what that silence meant. Lucky had thoughts which later he would claim had been too vague to talk about.

"Is one of the ergometers for me?" he asked.

"You bet," said Lucky, tossing one of the ergometers toward him. Bigman snatched it out of the air.

Hanley Cook was waiting for them when they stepped out of their quarters, wearing their suits but with headpieces tucked under their arms.

He said, "I thought I'd lead you as far as the nearest entrance to the shafts."

"Thank you," said Lucky.

It was the tail end of the sleeping period in the Dome. Human beings always established an Earth-like alternation of waking and sleeping, even where there was no day and night to guide them. Lucky had chosen this time on purpose, since he did not want to enter the mines at the head of a curious procession. In this Dr. Peverale had co-operated.

The corridors of the Dome were empty. The lighting was dimmed. And as they walked, a heavy silence seemed to fall about them while the clank of their footsteps sounded even louder.

Cook stopped. "This is Entry Two."

Lucky nodded. "All right. I hope we'll be seeing one another again soon."

"Right."

Cook operated the lock with his usual gloomy gravity, while Lucky and Bigman put on their headpieces, clamping them firmly along the paramagnetic seams. Lucky took his first breath of canned air with what was almost pleasure, he was so accustomed to it.

Lucky first, then Bigman, stepped into the air lock. The wall closed behind them.

Lucky said, "Ready, Bigman?"

"You bet, Lucky." His words rang in Lucky's radio receiver, and his small form was a shadow in the extremely dim light of the lock.

Then the opposing wall opened. They could feel the puff of air escaping into vacuum, and they stepped forward through the opening once again.

A touch at the outer controls and the wall closed behind them again. This time, light was shut off altogether.

Standing in absolute darkness, they found themselves inside the silent and empty mines of Mercury.

7

THE MINES OF MERCURY

THEY FLICKED ON THEIR SUIT-LIGHTS and the darkness was alleviated over a little space. They lit a tunnel that stretched out before them, dimly and more dimly and ending in darkness. The light beam had the usual sharp edge inevitable in a vacuum. Everything outside the direct beam remained completely black.

The tall man from Earth and his short companion from Mars faced that darkness and marched forward into the bowels of Mercury.

In the radiance of their suit-lights, Bigman looked curiously about at the tunnel, which resembled those he had seen on the Moon. Rounded out smoothly by the use of blasters and disintegrating procedures, it stretched out straight and even. The walls were curved and merged into the rocky ceiling. The oval cross section, slightly flattened above and quite flattened below, made for the greatest structural strength.

Bigman could hear his own steps through the air in his suit. He could sense Lucky's steps only as a small shock of vibration along rock. It was not quite sound, but to a person who had passed as much of his life in vacuum and near-vacuum as had Bigman it was almost as meaningful. He could "hear" the vibration of solid material much as ordinary Earthmen could hear the vibration of air which is called "sound."

Periodically they passed columns of rock which had been left unblasted and which served as buttresses for

the layers of rock between the tunnel and the surface.
Again this was like the mines on the Moon, except that
the buttresses were both thicker and more numerous
here, which was reasonable, since Mercury's gravity,
small as it was, was two and a half times that of the
Moon.

Tunnels branched off the main shaft along which
they traveled. Lucky, who seemed in no hurry, paused
at each opening in order to compare matters with the
chart he carried.

To Bigman, the most melancholy aspect of the mines
was the vestiges of one-time human occupancy: the bolts
where illumo-plates must once have been attached to
keep the corridors blazing with the light of day, the
faint markings where paramagnetic relays must once
have afforded traction for ore cars, occasional side
pockets where rooms or laboratories must have existed,
where miners might pause to eat at field kitchens or
where samples of ore might be assayed.

All dismantled now, all torn down, only bare rock
left.

But Bigman was not the man to brood overlong on
such matters. Rather, he grew concerned at the lack of
action. He had not come out here merely for the walk.

He said, "Lucky, the ergometer doesn't show a
thing."

"I know, Bigman. Cover."

He said it quietly, with no special emphasis, but
Bigman knew what it meant. He shoved his radio control to the particular notch which activated a shield for
the carrier wave and scrambled the message. It was not
regulation equipment on a space-suit, but it was routine
for Lucky and Bigman. Bigman had added the scram-
bler to the radio controls when preparing the suits
almost without giving the matter a conscious thought.

Bigman's heart was beating a little faster. When
Lucky called for a tight, scrambled beam between the
two of them, danger was near. Nearer, at any rate. He
said, "What's up, Lucky?"

"It's time to talk." Lucky's voice had a faintly far-off

sound, as though it was coming indeterminately from all directions. That was due to the inevitable lack of perfection of the part of the receiving unscrambler, which always left a small fraction of "noise."

Lucky said, "This is Tunnel 7a, according to the chart. It leads back by a fairly simple route to one of the vertical shafts leading to the surface. I'll be going there."

Bigman said, amazed, "You will? Why, Lucky?"

"To get to the surface," and Lucky laughed lightly. "Why else?"

"What for?"

"In order to travel along the surface to the hangar and the *Shooting Starr*. When I went to the ship last time, I took the new inso-suit with me."

Bigman chewed that over and said slowly, "Does that mean you'll be heading for Sun-side?"

"Right. I'll be heading for the big Sun. I can't get lost, at least, since I need only follow the coronal glow on the horizon. It makes it very simple."

"Come off it, Lucky, will you? I thought it was the mines that have the Sirians in them. Didn't you prove that at the banquet?"

"No, Bigman, I didn't prove it. I just fast-talked it into sounding as though it were proven."

"Then why didn't you say so to me?"

"Because we've argued this out before, I don't want to go into it. I can't risk your losing your temper at the wrong time. If I had told you our coming down here was part of a deeper plan and if, for any reason, Cook had irritated you, you might have blurted it right out."

"I would not, Lucky. It's just that you hate to say anything at all till you're all ready."

"There's that too," admitted Lucky. "Anyway, that's the situation. I wanted everyone to think I was going into the mines. I wanted everyone to think I hadn't the foggiest notion of heading for Sun-side. The safest way of seeing to it was to make sure nobody, but nobody, not even you, Bigman, thought any differently."

"Can you tell me why, Lucky? Or is that still all a big secret?"

"I can tell you this. I have a strong notion that someone at the Dome is behind the sabotage. I don't believe in the Sirian theory."

Bigman was disappointed. "You mean there's nothing down here in the mines?"

"I could be wrong. But I agree with Dr. Cook. It is just too unlikely that Sirius would put all the effort that would be involved in setting up a secret base on Mercury just to achieve a bit of sabotage. It would be much more likely that, if they wanted to do such a thing, they would bribe an Earthman to do it. After all, who slashed the inso-suit? That, at least, can't be blamed on Sirians. Even Dr. Peverale hasn't suggested there are Sirians inside the Dome."

"Then you're looking for a traitor, Lucky?"

"I'm looking for the saboteur. He may be a traitor in the pay of Sirius, or he may be working for reasons of his own. I hope the answer is on the Sun-side. And I hope, furthermore, that my smoke screen concerning an invasion of the mines will keep the guilty person from having time to cover up or from preparing an uncomfortable reception for me."

"What answer do you expect?"

"I'll know when I find it."

"Okay," said Bigman. "I'm sold, Lucky. On our way. Let's go."

"Hold on, there," cried Lucky in honest perturbation. "Great Galaxy, boy! I said *I'm* going. There's only one inso-suit. You'll stay here."

For the first time, the significance of the pronouns Lucky had used sank into Bigman's consciousness. Lucky had said "I," "I." Not once had he said "we." And yet Bigman, with the easy confidence of long association, had assumed that "I" meant "we."

"Lucky!" he cried, torn between outrage and dismay. "Why do I have to stay?"

"Because I want the men at the Dome to be sure that we're here. You keep the chart and follow the route we talked about or something like it. Report back to Cook every hour. Tell them where you are, what you see, tell the truth; you don't have to make anything up—except that you say I'm with you."

Bigman considered that. "Well, what if they want to talk to you?"

"Tell them I'm busy. Yell that you think you've just seen a Sirian. Say you've got to cut off. Make up something, but keep them thinking I'm here. See?"

"All right. Sands of Mars, you'll go to Sun-side and have all the fun, and I'll just wander around in the dark playing games on the suit radio."

"Cheer up, Bigman, there *may* be something in the mines. I'm not always right."

"I'll bet you are this time. There's *nothing* down here."

Lucky couldn't resist a joke. "There's the freezing death Cook spoke about. You could investigate that."

Bigman didn't see the humor. He said, "Aw, shut up."

There was a short pause. Then Lucky placed his hand on the other's shoulder. "All right, that wasn't funny, Bigman, and I'm sorry. Now cheer up, really. We'll be together again in no time. You know that."

Bigman pushed Lucky's arm to one side. "All right. Drop the soft soap. You say I've got to do it, so I'll do it. Only you'll probably get sunstroke without me there keeping an eye on you, you big ox."

Lucky laughed. "I'll try to be careful." He turned down tunnel 7a but had not taken two steps when Bigman called out.

"Lucky!"

Lucky stopped. "What?"

Bigman cleared his throat. "Listen. Don't take stupid chances, will you? I mean, I'm not going to be around to drag you out of trouble."

Lucky said, "Now you sound like Uncle Hector. Suppose you take some of your own advice, eh?"

It was as close as they ever got to expressing their real affection for one another. Lucky waved his hand

and stood glimmering for a moment in Bigman's suit-light. Then he turned and went off.

Bigman looked after him, following his figure as it gradually melted into the surrounding shadows until it turned about a curve in the tunnel and was lost to him.

He felt the silence, and the loneliness doubled. If he had not been John Bigman Jones, he might have weakened with the sense of loss, been overwhelmed at finding himself alone.

But he was John Bigman Jones, and he set his jaw and clamped his teeth and marched farther down the main shaft with unshaken tread.

Bigman made his first call to the Dome fifteen minutes later. He was miserable.

How could he have believed that Lucky seriously expected adventure in the mines? Would Lucky have arranged to make radio calls for the Sirians to pick up and keep tabs on?

Sure, it was a tight beam, but the messages weren't scrambled, and no beam was so tight that it couldn't be tapped with patience.

He wondered why Cook allowed such an arrangement, and almost at once the thought occurred to him that Cook disbelieved in the Sirians too. Only Bigman had believed. Big-brain!

At the moment, he could have chewed through a spaceship hull.

He gathered in Cook and used the agreed-upon signal for all clear.

Cook's voice at once shot back. "All clear?"

"Sands of Mars! Yes. Lucky's up ahead twenty feet, but there's no sign of anything. Look, if I've buzzed all clear, take my word for it next time."

"Let me talk to Lucky Starr."

"What for?" Bigman kept it casual with an effort. "Get him next time."

Cook hesitated, then said, "All right."

Bigman nodded to himself grimly. There'd be no next time. He'd buzz all clear and that would be all.

. . . Only how long was he supposed to wander about in the darkness before he heard from Lucky? An hour? Two? Six? Suppose six hours went by and there was no word? How long should he stay? How long *could* he stay?

And what if Cook demanded specific information? Lucky had said to describe things, but what if Bigman accidentally failed to keep up the act? What if he tipped the boat and let slip the fact that Lucky had gone into the Sun-side? Lucky would never trust him again! With anything!

He put the thought aside. It would do him no good to concentrate on it.

If there were only something to distract him. Something besides darkness and vacuum, besides the faint vibration of his own footsteps and the sound of his own breath.

He stopped to check his position in the main shaft. The side passages had letters and numbers ground sharply into their walls, and time had done nothing to dull their sharpness. Checking wasn't difficult.

However, the low temperature made the chart brittle and difficult to handle, and that didn't sweeten his mood. He turned his suit-light on his chest controls in order that he might adjust the dehumidifier. The inner surface of his face-plate was beginning to mist over faintly from the moisture in his breath, probably because the temperature within rose with his temper, he told himself.

He had just completed the adjustment when he moved his head sharply to one side as though he were suddenly cocking an ear to listen.

It was exactly what he was doing. He strained to sense the rhythm of faint vibration that he "heard" now only because his own steps had ceased.

He held his breath, remained as motionless as the rocky wall of the tunnel.

"Lucky?" he breathed into the transmitter. "Lucky?" The fingers of his right hand had adjusted the controls. The carrier wave was scrambled. No one else would make sense out of that light whisper. But Lucky would, and soon his voice would come in answer. Bigman was ashamed to admit to himself how welcome that voice would be.

"Lucky?" he said again.

The vibration continued. There was no answer.

Bigman's breathing quickened, first with tension, then with the savage joy born of excitement that always came over him when danger was in the offing.

There was someone else in the mines of Mercury with him. Someone other than Lucky.

Who, then? A Sirian? Had Lucky been right after all though he had thought he was merely putting up a smoke screen?

Maybe.

Bigman drew his blaster and put out his suit-light.

Did they know he was there? Were they coming to get him?

The vibrations weren't the blurred nonrhythmic "sound" of many people, or even two or three. To Bigman's keen ear, the distinctly separated "thrum-thrum" of vibration was the "sound" of one man's legs, rhythmically advancing.

And Bigman would meet any one man, anywhere, under any conditions.

Quietly, he put out his hand, touching the nearer wall. The vibrations sharpened noticeably. The other was in that direction then.

He moved forward quietly in the pitch-dark, his hand keeping a light touch on the wall. The vibrations being set up by the other were too intense, too careless. Either the other believed himself alone in the mines (as Bigman himself had until a moment before) or, if he were following Bigman, he wasn't wise in the ways of the vacuum.

Bigman's own footsteps had died to a murmur as he advanced catlike, yet the other's vibrations showed no change. Again, if the other had been following Bigman by sound, the sudden change in Bigman's progress should have been reflected in a change in the other's. It wasn't. The same conclusion, then as before.

He turned right at the next side-tunnel entrance and continued. His hand on the wall at once kept him along the way and guided him toward the other.

And then there was the blinding flash of a suit-light far ahead in the darkness as the motion of another's body whipped the beam across him. Bigman froze against the wall.

The light vanished. The other had passed across the tunnel Bigman was on. He was not advancing along it.

Bigman hurried forward lightly. He would find that cross tunnel and then he would be behind the other.

They would meet then. He, Bigman, representing Earth and the Council of Science, and the enemy representing—whom?

8

THE ENEMY IN THE MINES

BIGMAN HAD CALCULATED CORRECTLY. The other's light was bobbing along ahead of him, as he found the opening. Its owner was unaware of him. He *must* be.

Bigman's blaster was ready. He might have shot unerringly, but a blaster would not have left much behind. Dead men tell no tales and dead enemies explain no mysteries.

He pursued with catlike patience, cutting down the distance between them, following the light, trying to estimate the nature of the enemy.

His blaster always ready, Bigman moved to make first contact. First, radio! His fingers set the controls quickly for general local transmission. The enemy might have no equipment to receive that on the wave lengths Bigman could deliver. Unlikely, but possible! Very unlikely and barely possible!

Yet it didn't matter. There was always the alternative of a light blaster bolt against the wall. It would make his point clearly enough. A blaster carried authority and had a plain way of speaking that was understood in any language anywhere.

He said, his tenor voice carrying all the force it could muster, "Stop, you! Stop where you are and don't turn around! There's a blaster beaded in on you!"

Bigman flashed on his suit-light, and in its glare the enemy froze. Nor did he make any effort to turn

70

around, which was proof enough for Bigman that he had received the message.

Bigman said, "Now turn around. Slowly!"

The figure turned. Bigman kept his right hand in the path of his suit-light. Its metal sheath was clamped tightly about the large-caliber blaster. In the glow of the light, its outline was comfortingly clear.

Bigman said, "This blaster is fully charged. I've killed men with it before, and I'm a dead shot."

The enemy obviously had radio. He was obviously receiving, for he glanced at the blaster and made a motion as though to raise a hand to block off the blaster's force.

Bigman studied what he could see of the enemy's suit. It looked quite conventional (did the Sirians use such familiar models?).

Bigman said curtly, "Are you keyed in for radio transmission?"

There was sudden sound in his ears and he jumped. The voice was a familiar one, even under the disguising distortion of the radio; it said, "It's peewee, isn't it?"

Never in his life had Bigman needed greater self-control to keep from using his blaster.

As it was, the weapon leaped convulsively in his hand and the figure facing him leaned quickly to one side.

"Urteil!" yelled Bigman.

His surprise turned to disappointment. No Sirian! Only Urteil!

Then the sharp thought: What was Urteil doing here?

Urteil said, "It's Urteil all right. So put away the bean-shooter."

"That gets put away when I feel like it," said Bigman. "What are you doing here?"

"The mines of Mercury are not your private property, I think."

"While I have the blaster they are, you fat-faced cobber." Bigman was thinking hard and, to a certain extent, futilely. What was there to do with this poisonous skunk? To take him back to the Dome would reveal the fact that Lucky was no longer in the mines. Bigman could tell them that Lucky had lingered behind, but then they would become either suspicious or concerned when Lucky failed to report. And of what crime could he accuse Urteil? The mines were free to all, at that.

On the other hand, he could not remain indefinitely pointing a blaster at the man.

If Lucky were here, he would know—

And as though a telepathic spark had crossed the vacuum between the two men, Urteil suddenly said, "And where's Starr, anyway?"

"That," said Bigman, "is nothing you have to worry about." Then, with sudden conviction, "You were following us, weren't you?" and he shoved his blaster forward a little as though encouraging the other to talk.

In the glare of Bigman's suit-light, the other's glass-site-hidden face turned downward slightly as though to follow the blaster. He said, "What if I were?"

Again there was the impasse.

Bigman said, "You were going along a side passage You were going to swing in behind us."

"I said—— What if I were?" Urteil's voice had almost a lazy quality about it, as though its owner were thoroughly relaxed, as though he enjoyed having a blaster pointed at him.

Urteil went on. "But where's your friend? Near here?"

"I know where he is. No need for you to worry."

"I insist on worrying. Call him. Your radio is on local transmission or I wouldn't hear you so well. . . . Do you mind if I turn on my fluid jet? I'm thirsty." His hand moved slowly.

"Careful," said Bigman.

"Just a drink."

Bigman watched tensely. He did not expect a weapon to be activated by chest control, but the suit-light could be suddenly raised to blinding intensity, or—or —— Well, anything.

But Urteil's fingers finished their motion while Bigman stood irresolute, and there was only the sound of swallowing.

"Scare you?" asked Urteil calmly.

Bigman could find nothing to say.

Urteil's voice grew sharp. "Well, call the man. Call Starr!"

Under the impact of the order, Bigman's hand began a movement and stopped.

Urteil laughed. "You almost adjusted radio controls, didn't you? You needed distance tranmission. He's nowhere near here, is he?"

"No such thing," cried Bigman hotly. He was burning with mortification. The large and poisonous Urteil was clever. There he stood, the target of a blaster, yet winning the battle, proving himself master of the situation, while with every passing second Bigman's own position, in which he could neither shoot nor lower his blaster, leave nor stay, grew more untenable.

Wildly the thought gnawed at him: Why not shoot?

But he knew he could not. He would be able to advance no reason. And even if he could, the violent death of Senator Swenson's man would make tremendous trouble for the Council of Science. And for Lucky!

If only Lucky were here——

Partly because he wished that so ardently, his heart leaped as Urteil's light lifted slightly and focused beyond him, and he heard Urteil say, "No, I'm wrong after all and you're right. Here he comes."

Bigman whirled. "Lucky——"

In his right mind, Bigman would have waited calmly enough for Lucky to reach them, for Lucky's arm to be on his shoulder, but Bigman was not quite in his right mind. His position was impossible, his desire for a way out overwhelming.

He had time only for that one cry of "Lucky" before going down under the impact of a body fully twice as massive as his own.

For a few moments he retained the grip on his blaster, but another arm was tearing at his hand, strong fingers were wrenching and twisting his. Bigman's breath was knocked out of him, his brain was whirling with the suddenness of the attack, and his blaster went flying.

The weight lifted from him, and when he turned to struggle to his feet Urteil was towering over him and Bigman was staring into the muzzle of his own blaster.

"I have one of my own," said Urteil, grimly, "but I think I'd rather use yours. Don't move. Stay that way. On hands and knees. That's right."

Never in his life had Bigman so hated himself. To be tricked and hoodwinked this way. He almost deserved death. He would almost rather die than ever have to face Lucky and say, "He looked behind me and said you were coming so I turned——"

He said in a strangled voice, "Shoot, if you have the nerve for it. Shoot, and Lucky will track you down and see to it that you spend the rest of your life chained to the smallest, coldest asteroid ever used as a prison."

"Lucky will do that? Where is he?"

"Find him."

"I will because you'll tell me where he is. And tell me, too, why he came down to the mines in the first place. What's he doing here?"

"To find Sirians. You heard him."

"To find comet gas," growled Urteil. "That senile fool, Peverale, may talk Sirians, but your friend never believed any of it. Not even if he only has the brains you do. He came down for another reason. You tell me."

"Why should I?"

"To save your miserable life."

"That's not enough reason for me," said Bigman, and he rose to his feet and took a step forward.

Urteil moved backward till he was leaning against the wall of the tunnel. "One more motion and I'll blast you with pleasure. I don't need your information very badly. It will save time, but not much. If I spend more than five minutes with you, it's a waste.

"Now let me tell you exactly what I think. Maybe it

will teach you that you and your tin hero, Starr, are fooling nobody. Neither one of you is good for anything more than tricks with force-knives against an unarmed man."

Bigman thought gloomily: *That's* what's griping the cobber. I made him look like a jackass in front of the boys, and he's waiting for me to crawl.

"If you're going to do all that talking," he said, squeezing as much contempt into his voice as he could manage, "you might as well shoot. I'd rather be blasted than talked to death."

"Don't race for it, little fellow, don't race for it. In the first place, Senator Swenson is breaking the Council of Science. You're just an item, a tiny one. Your friend Starr is just another item, and not a much bigger one. I'm the one who's going to do the breaking. We've got the Council where we want it. The people of Earth know it's riddled with corruption, that its officers waste the taxpayers' money and line their own pockets——"

"That's a filthy lie," broke in Bigman.

"We'll let the people decide that. Once we puncture the phony propaganda the Council puts out, we'll see what the people think."

"You try that. Go ahead and try!"

"We intend to. We'll succeed too. And this will be exhibit number one: you two in the mines. I know why you're here. The Sirians! Huh! Starr either put Peverale up to telling the story, or he just took advantage of it. I'll tell you what you two are doing down here. You're faking the Sirians. You're setting up a Sirian camp to show people.

" 'I chased them off singlehanded,' Starr will say. 'I, Lucky Starr, big hero.' The sub-etherics make a big deal out of it and the Council calls off its Project Light on the sly. They've milked it for all it's worth, and they're getting out with their skins. . . . Except that they won't be because I'll catch Starr in the act and he'll be so much mud under shoe and so will the Council."

Bigman was sick with fury. He longed to tear at the other with his bare hands, but somehow he managed to hold himself in leash. He knew why Urteil was talking as he was. It was because the man *didn't* know as much as he pretended. He was trying to get more out of Bigman by making him blind-mad.

In a low voice, Bigman tried to turn the tables. "You know, you putrid cobber, if anyone ever punctured you and let out the comet gas, your peanut-sized soul would show itself clear. Once they let the rot out of you, you'd collapse to nothing but a loose sack of dirty skin."

Urteil shouted, "That's enough——"

But Bigman shouted over him, his high-pitched voice ringing. "Shoot, you yellow pirate. You showed yellow at the dinner table. Stand up to me, man to man, with bare fists and you'll show yellow again, bloated as you are."

Bigman was tense now. Let Urteil act in rash haste now. Let Urteil aim on impulse and Bigman would jump. Death was probable, but there would be a chance——

But Urteil seemed only to stiffen and grow colder.

"If you don't talk, I'll kill you. And nothing will happen to me. I'll claim self-defense and make it stick."

"Not with Lucky, you won't."

"He'll have his own troubles. When I'm through with him, his opinions won't mean a thing." The blaster in Urteil's hand was steady. "Are you going to try to run for it?"

"From you?" Bigman said.

"It's up to you," said Urteil coldly.

Bigman waited, waited without saying a word while Urteil's arm grew stiff and Urteil's headpiece dropped slightly as though he were taking aim, though at point-blank range he could not miss.

Bigman counted the moments, trying to choose the one in which to make his desperate jump for life as Lucky had when Mindes had similarly aimed at him. But here there was no second party to tackle Urteil as Bigman had tackled Mindes on that occasion. And

Urteil was no panicky, mind-sick Mindes. He would laugh and aim again.

Bigman's muscles tensed for that final jump. He did not expect to live for more than five more seconds, perhaps.

9

DARK AND LIGHT

BUT WITH HIS BODY TAUT, his leg muscles almost vibrating in the first part-instant of contraction, there was a sudden hoarse cry of utter surprise in Bigman's ears.

They were standing there, both of them, in a gray, dark world in which their beams of light etched one another out. Outside the beams of light, nothing, so that the sudden blob of motion that flashed across the line of sight made no sense at first.

His first reaction, his first thought was: Lucky! Had Lucky returned? Had he somehow mastered the situation, turned the tables?

But there was motion again, and the thought of Lucky faded away.

It was as though a fragment of the rocky wall of the shaft had worked itself loose and was drifting downward in the lazy fall that was characteristic of Mercury's low gravity.

A rope of rock that was somehow flexible, that struck Urteil's shoulder and—clung. One such encircled his waist already. Another moved slowly, bringing itself down and around as though it were part of an unreal world of slowed motion. But as its edge circled Urteil's arm and touched the metal covering Urteil's chest, arm and chest closed upon one another. It was as though the sluggish and seemingly brittle rock contained the irresistible strength of a boa constrictor.

If Urteil's first reaction had been one of surprise,

78

there was now nothing but complete terror in his voice.

"Cold," he croaked harshly. "They're cold."

Bigman's whirling mind was having trouble encompassing the new situation. A piece of that rock had encircled Urteil's lower arm and wrist. The butt of the blaster was clamped in place.

A final rope came floating down. They were so rocklike in appearance that they were invisible until one actually detached itself from the wall.

The ropes were connected one with another as a single organism, but there was no nucleus, no "body." It was like a stony octopus consisting of nothing but tentacles.

Bigman had a kind of explosion of thought.

He thought of rock developing life through the long ages of Mercurian evolution. A completely different form of life from anything Earth knew. A life that lived on scraps of heat alone.

Why not? The tentacles might crawl from place to place, seeking any bit of heat that might exist. Bigman could see them drifting toward Mercury's North Pole when mankind was first established there. First the mines and then the Observatory Dome supplied them with unending trickles of heat.

Man could be their prey too. Why not? A human being was a source of heat. Occasionally an isolated miner might have been trapped. Paralyzed with sudden cold and terror, he would be unable to call for help. Minutes later his power unit would be too low to make a radio call possible in any case. Still later, he would be dead, a frozen relic.

Cook's mad story of the deaths in the mines made sense.

All this passed through Bigman's mind almost in one flash while he remained unmoving, still struggling with a sense of stunned amazement at the sudden new turn of events.

Urteil's voice was somewhere between a moan and a harsh gasp. "I—can't—— Help me—help—— It's cold—cold——"

Bigman yelled, "Hold on. I'm coming."

Gone in a moment was any thought that this man was an enemy, that moments before he had been on the point of killing Bigman in cold blood. The little Martian recognized but one thing; here was a man, helpless in the grip of something nonhuman.

Since man had first left Earth and ventured into the dangers and mysteries of outer space, there had grown up a stern, unwritten law. Human feuds must be forgotten when man faced the common enemy, the nonhuman and inhuman forces of the other worlds.

It might be that not everyone adhered to that law, but Bigman did.

He was at Urteil's side in a bound, tearing at his arm.

Urteil mumbled, "Help me——"

Bigman grasped at the blaster Urteil still held, trying to avoid the tentacle that encircled Urteil's clutching fist. Bigman noted absently that the tentacle didn't curve smoothly like a snake would. It bent in sections as though arranged in numerous stiff segments hinged together.

Bigman's other hand, groping for purchase on Urteil's suit, made momentary contact with one of the tentacles and sprang away reflexively. The cold was an icy shaft, penetrating and burning his hand.

Whatever method the creatures had of withdrawing heat, it was like nothing he had ever heard of.

Bigman yanked desperately at the blaster, heaving and wrenching. He did not notice at first the alien touch on his back, then—iciness lay over him and did not go away. When he tried to jump away he found he could not. A tentacle had reached out for him and embraced him.

The two men might have grown together, so firmly were they bound.

The physical pain of the cold grew, and Bigman wrenched at the blaster like a man possessed. Was it giving?

Urteil's voice startled him as it murmured, "No use——"

Urteil staggered and then, slowly, under the weak pull of Mercury's gravity, he toppled over to one side, carrying Bigman with him.

Bigman's body was numb. It was losing sensation. He could scarcely tell whether he was still holding the muzzle of the blaster or not. If he was, was it yielding to his wild, sidewise wrenches, or was it a last gasp of wishful thinking?

His suit-light was dimming as his power-unit drained much of its energy into the voracious power-sucking ropes.

Death by freezing could not be far away.

Lucky, having left Bigman in the mines of Mercury, and having changed to an inso-suit in the quiet of the hangared *Shooting Starr,* stepped out onto the surface of Mercury and turned his face toward the "white ghost of the Sun."

For long minutes he stood motionless, taking in once again the milky luminescence of the Sun's corona.

Absently, as he watched, he flexed his smoothly-muscled limbs one at a time. The inso-suit worked more smoothly than an ordinary space-suit. That, combined with its lightness, lent it an unusual sensation of not being there altogether. In an environment obviously airless, it was disconcerting, but Lucky brushed aside any feeling of uneasiness he might have had and surveyed the sky.

The stars were as numerous and brilliant as in open space, and he paid them little attention. It was something else he wanted to see. It was two days now, standard Earth time, since he had last seen these skies. In two days, Mercury had moved one forty-fourth of the way along its orbit around the Sun. That meant over eight degrees of sky had appeared in the east and over eight degrees had disappeared in the west. That meant new stars could be seen.

New planets too. Venus and Earth ought both to have risen above the horizon in the interval.

And there they were. Venus was the higher of the two, a diamond-bright bit of white light, much more brilliant than it ever appeared to be on Earth. From Earth, Venus was seen at a disadvantage. It was between Earth and the Sun, so that when Venus was closest, Earth could see only its dark side. On Mercury, Venus could be seen at the full.

At the moment, Venus was thirty-three million miles from Mercury. At the closest, however, it could approach to within almost twenty million miles, and then keen eyes could actually see it as a tiny disk.

Even as it was, its light almost rivaled that of the corona, and, staring at the ground, Lucky thought he could make out a double shadow extending from his feet, one cast by the corona (a fuzzy one) and one by Venus (a sharp one). He wondered if, under ideal circumstances, there might not be a triple shadow, the third being cast by Earth itself.

He found Earth, too, without difficulty. It was quite near the horizon, and, though it was brighter than any star or planet in its own skies, it was pale in comparison to the glorious Venus. It was less brightly lit by its more distant Sun; it was less cloudy and therefore reflected less of the light it did give. Furthermore, it was twice as far from Mercury as Venus was.

Yet in one respect it was incomparably more interesting. Where Venus's light was a pure white, Earth's light was a blue-green glow.

And more than that, there was near it, just skirting the horizon, the smaller yellow light of Earth's Moon. Together, Earth and Moon made a unique sight in the skies of the other planets inside the orbit of Jupiter. A double planet, traveling majestically across the skies in each other's company, the smaller circling the larger in a motion which, against the sky, looked like a slow wobble from side to side.

Lucky stared at the sight perhaps longer than he should have, yet he could not help it. The conditions of his life took him far from his home planet on occasion, and that made it all the dearer to him. All the quadrillions of human beings throughout the Galaxy had originated on Earth. Through almost all of man's history, Earth had been his only home, in fact. What man could look on Earth's speck of light without emotion?

Lucky tore his eyes away, shaking his head. There was work to be done.

He set out with firm stride toward the coronal glow, skimming close to the surface as was proper in low gravity, keeping his suit-light on and his gaze fixed at the ground before him in order to guard against its rough unevenness.

He had an idea of what he might find, but it was purely a notion, backed as yet by no definite fact. Lucky had a horror of discussing such notions, which were sometimes nothing more than intuitions. He even disliked lingering on them in his own mind. There was too great a danger of growing used to the idea, of beginning to depend upon it as truth, of closing the mind unintentionally to alternate possibilities.

He had seen this happen to the ebullient, ready-to-believe, ready-to-act Bigman. He had watched vague possibilities become firm convictions in Bigman's mind more than once——

He smiled gently at the thought of the little bantam. Injudicious he might be, levelheaded never, but he was loyal and ablaze with fearlessness. Lucky would rather have Bigman at his side than a fleet of armored spacecruisers manned by giants.

He missed the gnome-faced Martian now, as he leaped flatly along the Mercurian terrain, and it was partly to wipe out that uncomfortable sensation that Lucky returned to thoughts of the problem at hand.

The trouble was that there were so many crosscurrents.

First, there was Mindes himself, nervous, unstable, unsure of himself. It had never been entirely settled, really, how far his attack on Lucky had been momentary madness and how far settled calculation. There was Gardoma, who was Mindes's friend. Was he a dedicated idealist caught up in the dream of Project Light, or was he with Mindes for purely practical reasons? If so, what were they?

Urteil, himself, was a main focus of disturbance. He was intent on ruining the Council, and the object of his main attack was Mindes. Yet his arrogance naturally spread hate of himself wherever he went. Mindes hated him, of course, and so did Gardoma. Dr. Peverale hated him in a much more restrained fashion. He would not even discuss the man with Lucky.

At the banquet, Cook had seemed to shrink from talking to Urteil, never let his eyes as much as move in his direction. Was this simply because Cook was anxious to avoid the sharp, flailing edge of Urteil's tongue, or were there more specific reasons?

Cook thought little of Peverale too. He was ashamed of the old man's preoccupation with Sirius.

And there was one question that remained to be answered aside from all these things. Who had slashed Lucky's inso-suit?

There were too many factors. Lucky had a line of thought that threaded through them, but as yet that line was weak. Again he avoided concentrating on that line. He must retain an open mind.

The ground was sloping upward and he had adjusted his stride to suit it automatically. So preoccupied was he with his thoughts that the sight that caught his eyes as he topped that rise found him unprepared and struck him with amazement.

The extreme upper edge of the Sun was above the broken horizon, yet not the Sun itself. Only the prominences that edged the Sun showed, a small segment of them.

The prominences were brilliant red in color, and one, in the very center of those visible, was made up of blazing streamers moving upward and outward with inching slowness.

Sharp and bright against the rock of Mercury, undimmed by atmosphere, unhazed by dust, it was a sight

of incredible beauty. The tongues of flame seemed to be
growing out of Mercury's dark crust as though the
planet's horizon were on fire or a volcano of more than
giant size had suddenly erupted and been trapped in
mid-blaze.

Yet those prominences were incomparably more than
anything that could have appeared on Mercury. The
one he watched, Lucky knew, was large enough to
swallow a hundred Earths whole, or five thousand Mer-
curies. And there it burned in atomic fire, lighting up
Lucky and all his surroundings.

He turned off his suit-light to see.

Those surfaces of the rocks that faced directly
toward the prominences were awash with ruddy light,
all other surfaces were black as coal. It was as though
someone had painted a bottomless pit with streaks of
red. Truly it was the "red ghost of the Sun."

The shadow of Lucky's hand on his chest made a
patch of black. The ground ahead was more treacher-
ous, since the patches of light that caught every fragment of unevenness fooled the eye into a false estimate
of the nature of the surface.

Lucky turned on his suit-light once again and moved
forward toward the prominences along the curve of
Mercury, the Sun rising six minutes of arc for every
mile he went.

That meant that in less than a mile, the body of the
Sun would be visible and he would be on Mercury's
Sun-side.

Lucky had no way of knowing then that at that
moment Bigman was facing death by freezing. His
thought as he faced the Sun-side was only this: There
lies the danger and the crux of the problem, and there
lies the solution too.

10

THE SUN-SIDE

MORE OF THE PROMINENCES WERE NOW VISIBLE. Their redness brightened. The corona did not vanish (there was no atmosphere to scatter the prominence light and wash out dimmer glows), but it seemed less important now. The stars were still out and would stay out, Lucky knew, even when Mercury's sun was full in the sky, but who could pay attention to them now?

Lucky ran forward eagerly in the steady stride which he could maintain for hours without feeling unduly tired. Under the circumstances, he felt he could have maintained such a stride even under Earth's gravity.

And then, with no warning, no premonitory glow in the sky, no hint from any atmosphere, *there was the Sun!*

Rather, there was a hairline that was the Sun. It was an unbearable line of light edging a notch of broken rock on the horizon, as though some celestial painter had outlined the gray stone in brilliant white.

Lucky looked backward. Across the uneven ground that lay behind him there were the splotches of prominence-red. But now, just at his feet, there was a wash of white, catching crystal formations in glinting highlights.

He moved onward again, and the line of light became first a small splotch and then a larger one.

The boundary of the Sun was clearly visible, lifting a bit above the horizon in its center, curving gently down on each side. The curve was awesomely flat to one whose eyes were accustomed to the curvature of Earth's Sun.

Nor did the Sun's blaze drown out the prominences which crawled along its edge like flaming red snake-hair. The prominences were all over the Sun, of course, but only at the edge could they be seen. On the Sun's face, they were lost amid the glare below.

And over all was the corona.

Lucky marveled, even as he watched, at the manner in which the inso-suit had been adapted to its purpose.

A glance at the edge of Mercury's Sun would have been blinding to unprotected eyes, blinding forever. The visible light was bad enough in its intensity, but it was the hard ultra-violet, unfiltered by atmosphere, that would have meant death to vision ... and to life itself, eventually.

Yet the glass of the inso-suit's face-plate was so arranged molecularly as to grow less transparent in direct proportion to the brightness of the light that fell upon it. Only a small fraction of a per cent of the Solar blaze penetrated the plate, and he could stare at the Sun without danger, almost without discomfort. Yet at the same time, the light of the corona and the stars came through undiminished.

The inso-suit protected him in other ways. It was impregnated with lead and bismuth, not enough so as to raise its weight unduly, but enough to block out ultraviolet and x-radiation from the Sun. The suit carried a positive charge to deflect most of the cosmic rays to one side. Mercury's magnetic field was weak, but Mercury was close to the Sun and the cosmic ray density was large. Still, cosmic rays are composed of positively-charged protons, and like charges repel like.

And, of course, the suit protected him against the heat, not only by its insulating composition but by its mirrorlike reflecting surface, a pseudo-liquid molecular layer that could be activated by a touch on the controls.

In fact, Lucky reflected, when the advantages of the inso-suit were considered, it seemed a pity that it was not standard protection under all conditions. Unfortunately, he realized, its structural weakness, as a result of lacking metal in real quantity, made it impractical for use except where protection against heat and radiation were paramount considerations.

Lucky was a mile into the Sun-side now and not conscious of undue heat.

This did not surprise him. To stay-at-homes who confined their knowledge of space to the sub-etheric thriller shows, the Sun-side of any airless planet was simply a solid mass of undeviating heat.

This was an oversimplification. It depended on how high the Sun was in the sky. From this point on Mercury, for instance, with only a portion of the Sun above the horizon, comparatively little heat reached the surface, and that little was spread over a lot of ground as the radiation struck almost horizontally.

The "weather" changed as one went deeper into the Sun-side and finally, when one reached that portion where the Sun was high in the sky, it was everything the sub-etherics said it was.

And besides, there were always the shadows. In the absence of air, light and heat traveled in a straight line. Neither could reach within the shadow except for small fractions which were reflected or radiated into it from neighboring sunlit portions. The shadows were therefore frosty cold and carbon black though the Sun was ever so hot and bright.

Lucky was growing more aware of these shadows. At first, after the upper line of Sun had appeared, the ground had been almost all shadow with only occasional patches of light. Now, as the Sun rose higher and higher, the light spread and coalesced until the shadows were distinct things hovering behind boulders and hills.

At one time Lucky deliberately plunged into the shadow of a rise of rock a hundred yards across, and it was as though for a long minute he were back on the dark-side. The heat of the Sun, which he had scarcely noticed while it beat upon him, became evident by its decrease in the shadow. All around the shadow the ground glimmered brightly in sunlight, but within the shadow his suit-light was necessary to guide his steps.

He could not help noticing the difference in the surfaces that were in the shadow from those in the light. For on the Sun-side, at least, Mercury did have a kind of atmosphere. Not one in the Earthly sense, no nitrogen, oxygen, carbon dioxide, or water vapor, nothing like that. On the Sun-side, however, mercury would boil in places. Sulfur would be liquid and so would a number of volatile compounds. Traces of the vapor of such substances would cling to Mercury's superheated surface. These vapors froze out in the shadows.

This was brought forcibly to Lucky's mind when his insulated fingers brushed over the dark surface of one outcropping and came away smeared with a frozen hoar of mercury, glittering in his suit-light. It changed quickly into clinging liquid droplets as he emerged into the Sun and then, more slowly, evaporated away.

Slowly, the Sun seemed to be getting hotter. That did not worry Lucky. Even if it grew uncomfortably hot, he could always dodge into a shadow to cool off when necessary.

Short-wave radiation was perhaps a more important consideration. Lucky doubted even that was serious in this short-term exposure. Workers on Mercury had a horror of radiation, because they were continually exposed to small amounts. Lucky recalled Mindes's emphasis on the fact that the saboteur he had seen had remained standing in the Sun. It was natural that Mindes should be disturbed at that. When exposure was chronic any lengthening of the time of exposure was foolish. In Lucky's own case, however, exposure would be short-term—he hoped.

He ran across patches of blackish ground that stood out somberly against Mercury's more general reddish gray. The reddish gray was familiar enough. It resembled the soil of Mars, a mixture of silicates with the addition of iron oxide, which gave it that ruddy tinge.

The black was more puzzling. Wherever it was the

ground was definitely hotter, since black absorbed more of the Sun's heat.

He bent as he ran and found the black areas crumbly rather than gritty. Some of it came up on the palm of his gauntlet. He looked at it. It might be graphite, it might be iron or copper sulfide. It might be any of a number of things, but he would have bet on its being some variety of impure iron sulfide.

He paused in the shadow of a rock, finally, and took stock. In an hour and a half, he estimated he had traveled some fifteen miles, judging from the fact that the Sun was just about entirely above the horizon now. (At the moment, he was more interested in sipping sparingly at the suit's supply of liquid nutrient mixture than in estimating distance, however.)

Somewhere to the left of him were cables of Mindes's Project Light. Somewhere to the right of him were others. Their exact location did not matter. They covered hundreds of square miles, and to wander aimlessly among them in search of a saboteur would have been foolish.

Mindes had tried it, hit or miss, and had failed. If the object or objects he had seen had indeed been the saboteur, there might have been a warning from inside the Dome. Mindes had made no secret of the fact that he was heading out to Sun-side.

Lucky had, however. There would be no warning, he hoped.

And he had a form of help Mindes had not had. He flipped his small ergometer out of the pouch he had placed it in. He held it before him in cupped palm, his suit-light playing full on it.

Once activated, its red signal-patch blazed with incredible fury when held out in the sunlight. Lucky smiled tightly and adjusted it. There was short-wave radiation from the Sun.

The flame died.

Patiently, then, Lucky stepped out into the sunlight and scanned the horizon in every direction. Where, if anywhere, was there a source of atomic power other than the Sun? He found an indication of the Dome, of course, but the light due to that region increased as he dipped the ergometer downward. The Dome's power plant was nearly a mile underground, and a twenty degree downward dip was required for maximum power where he stood.

He turned slowly, the ergometer held gingerly between the two forefingers of each hand in order that the opaque material of the suit should not block off the telltale radiation. Around a second time and a third.

It seemed to him that in one particular direction there had been the briefest of flashes—scarcely enough to see against the sunlight, really. Perhaps no more than the product of wishful thinking.

He tried again.

No mistake now!

Lucky sighted along the direction in which that glow had appeared and moved in that direction. He did not conceal from himself the fact that he might only be tracking down a patch of radioactive ore.

He caught his first glimpse of one of Mindes's cables nearly a mile farther on.

It was not a single cable at all, rather a web of cables, lying half buried in the ground. He followed it some hundreds of yards and came upon a square metal plate, about four feet on a side and polished to a high gloss. It reflected the stars as though it were a clear pool of water.

No doubt, thought Lucky, if he placed himself in the proper position he would find himself staring into the reflection of the Sun. He became aware that the plate was changing its angle of elevation, becoming less horizontal, more vertical. He looked away to see if it were shifting in such a way as to catch the Sun.

When he looked back he was amazed. The clear square was no longer clear. Instead, it was a dull black, so dull that not all the light of Mercury's Sun seemed to be able to brighten it.

Then, as he watched, that dullness trembled, broke, and fragmented.

It was bright again.

He watched it through three more cycles as the angle of elevation made it more and more vertical. First, incredible reflection; then, complete dullness. During the dullness, Lucky realized, light would be absorbed; during the glossiness, it would be reflected. The alternation in phase might be perfectly regular, or there might be a deliberate, irregular pattern. He could not linger to find out and, if he did, it was doubtful whether his knowledge of hyperoptics would be enough to enable him to understand the purpose of it all.

Presumably hundreds or even thousands of such squares, all connected by a network of cables and all powered from an atomic micropile inside the Dome, were absorbing and reflecting light in a set way at different angles to the Sun. Presumably, this, in some way, could force light energy through hyperspace in a controlled manner.

And, presumably, torn cables and smashed plates prevented the over-all pattern from being properly completed.

Lucky tried his ergometer again. It was much brighter now, and again he followed in the indicated direction.

Brighter, brighter! Whatever it was he was following, it was something that was changing its position. The source of gamma rays was not a fixed point on Mercury's surface.

And *that* meant it was not merely an outcropping of radioactive ore. It was something portable, and to Lucky that meant it was man or something belonging to man.

Lucky saw the figure first as a moving speck, black against the fire-lit ground. The sight came after a long spell in the open Sun, at a time when he had been about to find himself a shadow in which to let the slowly accumulating heat drain away.

Instead, he accelerated his pace now. He estimated the temperature outside his suit to be at not quite the boiling point of water. Inside, fortunately, it was considerably lower.

He thought grimly: If the Sun were overhead and not at the horizon, even these suits would be of no use.

The figure paid no attention to him. It continued on its own path, its gait showing it far from as expert in handling low gravity as was Lucky. Indeed its motion might almost be described as lumbering. Yet it managed to devour space. It covered the ground.

It wore no inso-suit. Even at long distance, the surface exposed to Lucky's gaze was obviously one of metal.

Lucky paused briefly in the shade of a rock but forced himself out into the open again before there was time for much cooling.

The figure seemed unbothered by the heat. At least, in the time Lucky watched him he made no move to enter shadows, though he passed within a few feet of some.

Lucky nodded thoughtfully. It all fit well.

He sped on. The heat was beginning to feel like something he could touch and squeeze. But it would only be a few moments now.

He had abandoned his low-slung lope now. Every bit of his muscular power was being put into giant strides of up to fifteen feet each.

He shouted, "You! You there! Turn around!"

He said it peremptorily, with all the authority he could produce, hoping that the other could receive his radio signal and that he would not be reduced to sign language.

Slowly the figure turned, and Lucky's nostrils flared in a kind of cold satisfaction. So far, at least, it was as he thought, for the figure was no man—nothing human at all!

11

SABOTEUR!

THE FIGURE WAS TALL, taller even than Lucky. It was nearly seven feet tall, in fact, and broad in proportion. All of the figure that met the eye was gleaming metal, brilliant where it caught the Sun's rays, black with shadow where it did not.

But underneath that metal was no flesh and blood, only more metal, gears, tubes, a micropile which powered the figure with nuclear energy and produced the gamma rays that Lucky had detected with his pocket ergometer.

The limbs of the creature were monstrous and its legs were straddled far apart as it stood there facing Lucky. What passed for its eyes were two photoelectric cells that gleamed a deep red. Its mouth was a slash across the metal on the lower part of its face.

It was a mechanical man, a robot, and it took Lucky no more than one glance to know that it was no robot of Earth's manufacture. Earth had invented the positronic robot, but it had never built any model like this.

The robot's mouth opened and closed in irregular movements as though it were speaking.

Lucky said, "I cannot hear sound in a vacuum, robot." He said it sternly, knowing that it was essential to establish himself as a man and therefore a master at once. "Switch to radio."

And now the robot's mouth remained motionless but a voice sounded in Lucky's receiver, harsh and uneven, with the words unnaturally spaced. It said, "What is your business, sir? Why are you here?"

"Do not question me," said Lucky. "Why are *you* here?"

A robot could only be truthful. It said, "I have been instructed to destroy certain objects at intervals."

"By whom?"

"I have been instructed not to answer that question."

"Are you of Sirian manufacture?"

"I was constructed on one of the planets of the Sirian Confederation."

Lucky frowned. The creature's voice was quite unpleasant. The few robots of Earth manufacture that Lucky had had occasion to see in experimental laboratories had been outfitted with voice boxes which, by direct sound or by radio, seemed as pleasant and natural as a well-cultivated human voice. Surely the Sirians would have improved on that.

Lucky's mind shifted to a more immediate problem. He said, "I must find a shadowed area. Come with me."

The robot said at once, "I will direct you to the nearest shade." It set off at a trot, its metal legs moving with a certain irregularity.

Lucky followed the creature. He needed no direction to reach the shade, but he lagged behind to watch the robot's gait.

What had seemed to Lucky, from a distance, to be a lumbering or a clumsy pace, turned out, at close hand, to be a pronounced limp. A limp and a harsh voice. Two imperfections in this robot whose outer appearance was that of a magnificent mechanical marvel.

It struck him forcibly that the robot might not be adjusted to the heat and radiation of Mercury. Exposure had damaged it, probably. Lucky was scientist enough to feel a twinge of regret at that. It was too beautiful to have to endure such damage.

He regarded the machine with admiration. Underneath that massive skull of chrome-steel was a delicate ovoid of sponge platinum-iridium about the size of a human brain. Within it, quadrillions of quadrillions of positrons came into being and vanished in millionths of a second. As they came into being and vanished they traced precalculated paths which duplicated, in a simplified way, the thinking cells of the human brain.

Engineers had calculated out those positronic paths to suit humanity, and into them they had designed the "Three Laws of Robotics."

The First Law was that a robot could not harm a human being or let one come to harm. Nothing came ahead of that. Nothing could substitute for it.

The Second Law was that a robot must obey orders except those that would break the First Law.

The Third Law allowed a robot to protect itself, provided the First and Second Laws weren't broken.

Lucky came out of his short reverie when the robot stumbled and almost fell. There was no unevenness in the ground that Lucky could see, no trifling ridge that might have caught his toe. If there had been, a line of black shadow would have revealed it.

The ground was table-smooth at that point. The robot's stride had simply broken for no reason and thrown him to one side. The robot recovered after threshing about wildly. Having done that, it resumed its stride toward the shade as though nothing had happened.

Lucky thought: It's definitely in poor working order.

They entered the shadow together, and Lucky turned on his suit-light.

He said, "You do wrong to destroy necessary equipment. You are doing harm to men."

There was no emotion in the robot's face; there could be none. Nor was there emotion in its voice. It said, "I am obeying orders."

"That is the Second Law," said Lucky severely. "Still, you may not obey orders that harm human beings. That would be to violate the First Law."

"I have not seen any men. I have harmed no one."

"You have harmed men you did not see. I tell you that."

"I have harmed no man," said the robot stubbornly, and Lucky frowned at the unthinking repetition. Despite its polished appearance, perhaps it was not a very advanced model.

The robot went on. "I have been instructed to avoid men. I have been warned when men were coming, but I was not warned about you."

Lucky stared out past the shadow at the glittering Mercurian landscape, ruddy and gray for the most part but blotched with a large area of the crumbly black material which seemed so common in this part of Mercury. He thought of Mindes spotting the robot twice (his story made sense now) and losing it when he tried to get closer. His own secret invasion of the Sun-side, combined with the use of an ergometer, had turned the trick, fortunately.

He said suddenly and forcefully, "*Who* warned you to avoid men?"

Lucky didn't really expect to catch the robot. A robot's mind is machinery, he thought. It cannot be tricked or fooled, any more than you can trick a suit-light into going on by jumping at the switch and pretending to close contact.

The robot said, "I have been instructed not to answer that question." Then slowly, creakily, as though the words were coming out against its will, it said, "I do not wish you to ask such questions any longer. They are disturbing."

Lucky thought: To break the First Law would be more disturbing still.

Deliberately he stepped out of the shadow into the sunlight.

He said to the robot, who followed, "What is your serial number?"

"RL-726."

"Very well, RL-726, you understand I am a man?"

"Yes."

"I am not equipped to withstand the heat of Mercury's Sun."

"Nor am I," said the robot.

"I realize that," said Lucky, thinking of the robot's near-fall a few minutes earlier. "Nevertheless, a man is much less equipped for it than is a robot. Do you understand that?"

"Yes."

"Now, then, listen. I want you to stop your destructive activities, and I want you to tell me who ordered you to destroy equipment."

"I am instructed——"

"If you do not obey me," said Lucky loudly, "I will remain here in the Sun until I am killed and you will have broken the First Law, since you would have allowed me to be killed when you could have stopped it."

Lucky waited grimly. A robot's statement could not be accepted as evidence, of course, in any court, but it would assure him that he was on the right track if it were to say what he expected it to.

But the robot said nothing. It swayed. One eye blinked out suddenly (more imperfection!) then came to life. It's voice sounded in a wordless squawk, then it said in an almost drunken mumble, "I will carry you to safety."

"I would resist," said Lucky, "and you would have to harm me. If you answer my question, I will return to the shade of my own accord, and you will have saved my life without any damage to me at all."

Silence.

Lucky said, "Will you tell me who ordered you to destroy equipment?"

And suddenly the robot lunged forward, coming to within two feet of Lucky before stopping. "I told you not to ask that question."

Its hands moved forward as though to seize Lucky but did not complete the motion.

Lucky watched grimly and without concern. A robot could not harm a human being.

But then the robot lifted one of those mighty hands and put it to its head, for all the world as though it were a man with a headache.

Headache!

A sudden thought stabbed at Lucky. Great Galaxy! He'd been blind, stupidly, criminally blind!

It wasn't the robot's legs that were out of order, nor its voice, nor its eyes. How could the heat affect them? It was—it had to be—the positronic brain itself that was affected; the delicate positronic brain subjected to the direct heat and radiation of the Mercurian Sun for how long? Months?

That brain must be partially broken down already.

If the robot had been human, one would say he was in one of the stages of mental breakdown. One might say he was on the road to insanity.

A mad robot! Driven mad by heat and radiation!

How far would the Three Laws hold in a broken-down positronic brain?

And now Lucky Starr stood there, threatening a robot with his own death, while that same robot, nearly mad, advanced toward him, arms outstretched.

The very dilemma in which Lucky had placed the robot might be adding to that madness.

Cautiously, Lucky retreated. He said, "Do you feel well?"

The robot said nothing. Its steps quickened.

Lucky thought: If it's ready to break the First Law, it must be on the point of complete dissolution. A positronic brain would have to be in pieces to be capable of that.

Yet, on the other hand, the robot had endured for months. It might endure for months more.

He talked in a desperate attempt to delay matters and allow time for more thought.

He said, "Does your head ache?"

"Ache?" said the robot. "I do not understand the meaning of the word."

Lucky said, "I am growing warm. We had better retire to the shadow."

No more talk of heating himself to death. He retreated at a half-run now.

The robot's voice rumbled. "I have been told to prevent any interference with the orders given me."

Lucky reached for his blaster and he sighed. It would be unfortunate if he were forced to destroy the robot. It was a magnificent work of man, and the Council could investigate its workings with profit. And to destroy it without even having obtained the desired information was repugnant to him.

Lucky said, "Stop where you are."

The robot's arms moved jerkily as it lunged, and Lucky escaped by a hair as he floated away in a sidewise twist, taking the fullest advantage of Mercury's gravity.

If he could maneuver his way into the shadow; if the robot followed him there——

The coolness might calm those disordered positronic paths. It might become tamer, more reasonable, and Lucky might be spared the necessity of its destruction.

Lucky dodged again, and again the robot rushed past, its metal legs kicking up spurts of black grit that settled back to Mercury promptly and cleanly since there was no atmosphere to keep it in suspension. It was an eerie chase, the tread of man and robot hushed and silent in the vacuum.

Lucky's confidence grew somewhat. The robot's movements had grown jerkier. Its control of the gears and relays that manipulated its limbs was imperfect and growing more so.

Yet the robot was making an obvious attempt to head him off from the shadow. It was definitely and beyond any doubt trying to kill him.

And still Lucky could not bring himself to use the blaster.

He stopped short. The robot stopped too. They were face to face, five feet apart, standing on the black patch of iron sulfide. The blackness seemed to make the heat all the greater and Lucky felt a gathering faintness. The robot stood grimly between Lucky and the shade.

Lucky said, "Out of my way." Talking was difficult.

The robot said, "I have been told to prevent any

interference with the orders given me. You have been interfering."

Lucky no longer had a choice. He had miscalculated. It had never occurred to him to doubt the validity of the Three Laws under all circumstances. The truth had come to him too late, and his miscalculation had brought him to this: the danger of his own life and the necessity of destroying a robot.

He raised his blaster sadly.

And almost at once he realized that he had made a second miscalculation. He had waited too long, and the accumulation of heat and weariness had made his body as imperfect a machine as was the robot's. His arm lifted sluggishly, and the robot seemed to be twice life-sized to his own reeling mind and sight.

The robot was a blur of motion, and this time Lucky's tired body could not be driven into quick enough movement. The blaster was struck from Lucky's hand and went flying. Lucky's arm was clamped tight in the grip of one metal hand, and his waist was embraced by a metal arm.

Under the best of circumstances, Lucky could not have withstood the steel muscles of the mechanical man. No human being could have. Now he felt all capacity for resistance vanish. He felt only the heat.

The robot tightened its grip, bending Lucky backward as though he were a rag doll. Lucky thought dizzily of the structural weakness of the inso-suit. An ordinary space-suit might have protected him even against a robot's strength. An inso-suit could not. Any moment, a section of it might buckle and give.

Lucky's free arm flailed helplessly, his fingers dragging into the black grit below.

One thought flicked through his mind. Desperately he tried to drive his muscles into one last attempt to fend off what seemed inevitable death at the hands of a mad robot.

12

PRELUDE TO A DUEL

LUCKY'S PREDICAMENT WAS A DUPLICATE in reverse of
that which had faced Bigman some hours previously.
Bigman had been threatened not by heat but by
growing cold. He was held in the grip of the stony
"ropes" as firmly as Lucky in the grip of the metal
robot. In one respect, though, Bigman's position held
hope. His numbing grasp held desperately on the blaster pinned in Urteil's hand.

And the blaster was coming loose. In fact, it came
free so suddenly that Bigman's numbed fingers nearly
dropped it.

"Sands of Mars!" he muttered, and held on.

If he had known where in the tentacles a vulnerable
spot might be, if he could have blasted any part of
those tentacles without killing either Urteil or himself,
his problem would have been simple. As it was, there
was only one gamble, not a good one either, open to
him.

His thumb worked clumsily on the intensity control,
pushing it down and down. He was getting drowsy,
which was a bad sign. It had been minutes since he had
heard any sign of life from Urteil.

He had intensity at minimum now. One more thing;
he must reach the activator with his forefinger without
dropping the blaster.

Space! He mustn't drop it.

The forefinger touched the proper spot and pushed against it.

The blaster grew warm. He could see that in the dull red glow of the grid across the muzzle. That was bad for the grid since a blaster was not designed to be used as a heat ray, but to deep Space with that.

With what strength was left him, Bigman tossed the blaster as far as he could.

It seemed to him then as though reality wavered for a moment, as though he were on the edge of unconsciousness.

Then he felt the first glow of warmth, a tiny leakage of heat entering his body from the laboring power-unit, and he shouted in weak joy. That heat was enough to show that power was no longer being drained directly into the voracious bodies of the heat-sucking tentacles.

He moved his arms. He lifted a leg. They were free. The tentacles were gone.

His suit-light had brightened, and he could see clearly the spot where the blaster had been thrown. The spot, but not the blaster. Where the blaster should be was a sluggishly moving mass of gray, intertwining tentacles.

With shaky motions, Bigman snatched at Urteil's own blaster, setting it to minimum and tossing it past the position of the first. That would hold the creature if the energy of the first gave out.

Bigman said urgently, "Hey, Urteil. Can you hear me?"

There was no answer.

With what strength he could muster he pulled the space-suited figure away with him. Urteil's suit-light glimmered, and his power-unit gauge showed itself as not quite empty. The temperature inside his suit should return to normal quickly.

Bigman called the Dome. There was no other decision possible now. In their weakened condition, with their power supply low, another encounter with Mercurian life would kill them. And he would manage to protect Lucky's position somehow.

It was remarkable how quickly men reached them.

With two cups of coffee and a hot meal inside him and the Dome's light and heat all about him, Bigman's resilient mind and body put the recent horror into proper perspective. It was already only an unpleasant memory.

Dr. Peverale hovered about him with an air partly like that of an anxious mother, partly like that of a nervous old man. His iron-gray hair was in disarray. "You're sure you're all right, Bigman. No ill effects?"

"I feel fine. Never better," insisted Bigman. "The question is, Doc, how's Urteil?"

"Apparently he'll be all right." The astronomer's voice grew cold. "Dr. Gardoma has examined him and reported favorably on his condition."

"Good," said Bigman almost gloatingly.

Dr. Peverale said with some surprise, "Are you concerned for him?"

"You bet, Doc. I've plans for him."

Dr. Hanley Cook entered now, almost trembling with excitement. "We've sent men into the mines to see if we can round up any of the creatures. They're taking heating pads with them. Like bait to a fish, you know." He turned to Bigman. "Lucky you got away."

Bigman's voice rose in pitch and he looked outraged. "It wasn't luck, it was brains. I figured they were after straight heat most of all. I figured it was their favorite kind of energy. So I gave it to them."

Dr. Peverale left after that, but Cook remained behind, talking of the creatures, walking back and forth, bubbling with speculation. "Imagine! The old stories about the freezing death in the mines were true. Really true! Think of it! Just rocky tentacles acting as heat sponges, absorbing energy wherever they can make contact. You're sure of the description, Bigman?"

"Of course I'm sure. When you catch one, see for yourself."

"What a discovery."

"How come they were never discovered before?" asked Bigman.

"According to you, they blend into their environment. Protective mimicry. Then, too, they attack only isolated men. Maybe," his words grew quicker, more animated, and his long fingers intertwined and twisted with one another, "there is some instinct there, some rudimentary intelligence that kept them hidden and out of sight. I'm sure of it. It's a kind of intelligence that kept them out of our way. They knew their only safety was in obscurity, so they attack only single, isolated men. Then for thirty years or more no men appeared in the mines. Their precious kernels of unusual heat were gone, and yet they never succumbed to the temptation to invade the Dome itself. But when men finally appeared once more in the mines, *that* temptation was too great and one of the creatures attacked, even though there were two men there and not one. For them, that was fatal. They have been discovered."

"Why don't they go to the Sun-side if they want energy and they're all that intelligent?" demanded Bigman.

"Maybe that's too hot," said Cook at once.

"They took the blaster. It was red hot."

"The Sun-side may be too full of hard radiation. They may not be adapted to that. Or maybe there is another breed of such creature on the Sun-side. How can we know? Maybe the dark-side ones live on radioactive ores and on the coronal glow."

Bigman shrugged. He found such speculation unprofitable.

And Cook's line of thought seemed to change too. He stared speculatively at Bigman, one finger rubbing his chin rhythmically. "So you saved Urteil's life."

"That's right."

"Well, maybe it's a good thing. If Urteil had died, they would have blamed you. Senator Swenson could have made it darned hot for you and for Starr *and* for the Council. No matter what explanation you gave, you

would have been there when Urteil died, and that
would have been enough for Swenson."

"Listen," said Bigman, moving about uneasily,
"when do I get to see Urteil?"

"Whenever Dr. Gardoma says you may."

"Get him on the wire and tell him to say I can,
then."

Cook's gaze remained fastened thoughtfully on the
small Martian. "What's on your mind?"

And because Bigman had to make arrangements
about the gravity, he explained some of his plan to
Cook.

Dr. Gardoma opened the door and nodded to Bigman to enter. "You can have him, Bigman," he whis-
pered. "I don't want him."

He stepped out, and Bigman and Urteil were alone
with one another once again.

Jonathan Urteil was a little pallid where stubble
didn't darken his face, but that was the only sign of his
ordeal. He bared his lips in a savage grin. "I'm in one
piece, if that's what you've come to see."

"That's what I've come to see. Also to ask you a
question. Are you still full of that drivel about Lucky
Starr setting up a fake Sirian base in the mines?"

"I intend to prove it."

"Look, you cobber, you know it's a lie, and you're
going to fake proof if you can. *Fake* it! Now I'm not
expecting you to get on your knees to thank me for
saving your life——"

"Wait!" Slowly Urteil's face flushed. "All I remember is that that thing got me first by surprise. That was
accident. After that, I don't know what happened.
What *you* say means nothing to me."

Bigman shrieked with outrage. "You smudge of
space dust, you yelled for help."

"Where's your witness? I don't remember a thing."

"How do you suppose you got out?"

"I'm not supposing anything. Maybe the thing
crawled away on its own. Maybe there was no thing at

all. Maybe a rockfall hit me and knocked me out. Now if you came here expecting me to cry on your shoulders and promise to lay off your grafting friend, you're going to be disappointed. If you have nothing else to say, good-by."

Bigman said, "There's something you're forgetting. You tried to kill me."

"Where's your witness? Now if you don't get out, I'll pucker up and blow you out, midget."

Bigman remained heroically calm. "I'll make a deal with you, Urteil. You've made every threat you can think of because you're half an inch taller than I am and half a pound heavier, but you crawled the only time I made a pass at you."

"With a force-knife and myself unarmed. Don't forget that."

"I say you're yellow. Meet me rough and tumble, *now*. No weapons. Or are you too weak?"

"Too weak for you? Two years in the hospital and I wouldn't be too weak for you!"

"Then fight! Before witnesses! We can use the space in the power room. I've made arrangements with Hanley Cook."

"Cook must hate you. What about Peverale?"

"Nobody asked him. And Cook doesn't hate me."

"He seems anxious to get you killed. But I don't think I'll give him the satisfaction. Why should I fight a half-pint of skin and wind?"

"Yellow?"

"I said, why? You said you were making a deal."

"Right. You win, I don't say a word about what happened in the mines, what really happened. I win, you lay off the Council."

"Some deal. Why should I worry about anything you can say about me?"

"You're not afraid of losing, are you?"

"Space!" The exclamation was enough.

Bigman said, "Well, then?"

"You must think I'm a fool. If I fight with you before witnesses I'll be indicted for murder. If I lean a finger on you, you're squashed. Go find yourself another way to commit suicide."

"All right. How much do you outweigh me?"

"A hundred pounds," said Urteil contemptuously.

"A hundred pounds of fat," squeaked Bigman, his gnomish face screwed into a ferocious scowl. "Tell you what. Let's fight under Mercurian gravity. That makes your advantage forty pounds. And you keep your inertia advantage. Fair enough?"

Urteil said, "Space, I'd like to give you one smash, just to plaster your big mouth over your miserable little face."

"You've got your chance. Is it a deal?"

"By Earth, it's a deal. I'll try not to kill you, but that's as far as I'll go. You've asked for this, you've begged for it."

"Right. Now let's go. Let's go." And Bigman was so anxious that he hopped about as he talked, sparring a little with rapid birdlike motions of his fists. In fact, such was his eagerness for this duel that not once did he give a specific thought to Lucky nor suffer any presentiment of disaster. He had no way of telling that, some time before, Lucky had fought a more deadly duel than the one Bigman now proposed.

The power-level had its tremendous generators and heavy equipment, but it also had its broad level space suitable for gatherings of personnel. It was the oldest part of the Dome. In the first days, before even a single mine shaft had been blasted into Mercurian soil, the original construction engineers had slept on cots in that space between the generators. Even now it was still occasionally used for trifilm entertainment.

Now it served as a ring, and Cook, together with half a dozen or so technicians, remained dubiously on the side lines.

"Is this all?" demanded Bigman.

Cook said, "Mindes and his men are out Sun-side. There are ten men in the mines looking for your ropes, and the rest are mostly at their instruments." He looked apprehensively at Urteil and said, "Are you sure you know what you're doing, Bigman?"

Urteil was stripped to the waist. He had a thick growth of hair over his chest and shoulders, and he moved his muscles with an athletic joy.

Bigman looked in Urteil's direction indifferently. "All set with the gravity?"

"We'll have it off at the signal. I've rigged the controls so the rest of the Dome won't be affected. Has Urteil agreed?"

"Sure." Bigman smiled. "It's all right, pal."

"I hope so," said Cook fervently.

Urteil called out, "When do we get started?" Then, looking about the small group of spectators, he asked, "Anyone care to bet on the monkey?"

One of the technicians looked at Bigman with an uneasy grin. Bigman, now also stripped to his waist, looked surprisingly wiry, but the difference in size gave the match a grotesque appearance.

"No bet here," said the technician.

"Are we ready?" called Cook.

"I am," said Urteil.

Cook licked his pale lips and flicked the master switch. There was a change in the pitch of the subdued droning of the generators.

Bigman swayed with the sudden loss of wieght. So did all the rest. Urteil stumbled but recovered rapidly and advanced gingerly into the middle of the clear space. He did not bother to lift his arms but stood waiting in a posture of complete relaxation.

"Start something, bug," he said.

13

RESULTS OF A DUEL

FOR HIS PART, BIGMAN ADVANCED with gentle movements of his legs that translated themselves into slow and graceful steps, almost as though he were on springs.

In a way he was. Mercurian surface gravity was almost precisely equal to Martian surface gravity, and it was something he was at home with thoroughly. His cool, gray eyes, watching sharply, noticed every sway in Urteil's body, every knotting of a sudden muscle as he worked to keep erect.

Small misjudgments even in merely keeping one's balance were inevitable when working in a gravity to which one was unaccustomed.

Bigman moved in suddenly, springing from foot to foot and side to side in a broken motion that was at once amusingly dancelike and completely confusing.

"What is this?" growled Urteil in exasperation. "A Martian waltz?"

"Kind of," said Bigman. His arm lunged outward, and his bare knuckles slammed into Urteil's side with a resounding thwack, staggering the big fellow.

There was a gasp from the audience and one yell of "Hey, *boy!*"

Bigman stood there, arms akimbo, waiting for Urteil to recover his balance.

Urteil did so in a matter of five seconds, but now

there was an angry red splotch on his side and a similar and angrier one on each cheekbone.

His own arm shot out powerfully, his right palm half open as though a slap would be sufficient to fling this stinging insect out of his way forever.

But the blow continued, dragging Urteil about. Bigman had ducked, leaving a fraction of an inch to spare, with the sure judgment of a perfectly co-ordinated body. Urteil's efforts to stop his follow-through left him teetering wildly, back to Bigman.

Bigman placed his foot on the seat of Urteil's pants and shoved gently. The recoil sent him hopping easily backward on the other foot, but Urteil went slowly forward on his face in grotesque slow motion.

There was sudden laughter from the side lines.

One of the spectators called out, "Changed my mind, Urteil. I'm betting."

Urteil made no gesture of hearing this. He was facing Bigman again, and from the corner of his thick lips a viscid drop of saliva made its way down the corner of his chin.

"Up the gravity!" he roared hoarsely. "Get it to normal!"

"What's the matter, tubbo?" mocked Bigman. "Isn't forty pounds in your favor enough?"

"I'll kill you. I'll kill you," Urteil shouted.

"Go ahead!" Bigman spread his arms in mock invitation.

But Urteil was not entirely beyond reason. He circled Bigman, hopping a little in ungainly fashion. He said, "I'll get my gravity legs, bug, and once I grab you anywhere, that piece gets torn off you."

"Grab away."

But there was an uneasy silence among the men who watched now. Urteil was a stooping barrel, his arms sweeping out and wide, his legs spread. He was keeping his balance, catching the rhythm of the gravity.

Bigman was a slender stalk in comparison. He might be as graceful and self-assured as a dancer, yet he looked pitifully small.

Bigman seemed unworried. He hopped forward with a sudden stamp of his feet that sent him shooting high in the air, and when Urteil lunged at the rising figure, Bigman lifted his feet and was down behind his adversary before the other could turn around.

There was loud applause, and Bigman grinned.

He performed what was almost a pirouette as he ducked under one of the great arms that threatened him, reaching out and bringing the side of his hand sharply down against the biceps.

Urteil restrained a cry and whirled again.

Urteil maintained a dreadful calm to all these grandstanding provocations now. Bigman, on the other hand, tried in every way he could to taunt and sting Urteil into a wild motion that would send him shooting off balance.

Forward and away; quick, sharp blows, which for all their flicking qualities carried a sting.

But a new respect for Urteil was growing in the small Martian's mind. The cobber was taking it. He was maintaining his ground like a bear warding off the attack of a hunting dog. And Bigman was the hunting dog which could only hover at the outskirts, snap, snarl, and keep out of the reach of the bear's paws.

Urteil even looked like a bear with his large, hairy body, his small, bloodshot eyes, and his jowly, bristly face.

"Fight, cobber," jeered Bigman. "I'm the only one giving the customers a show."

Urteil shook his head slowly. "Come closer," he said.

"Sure," said Bigman lightly, dashing in. With flashing movements, he caught Urteil on the side of the jaw and was under his arm and away in almost the same movement.

Urteil's arm half moved, but it was too late and the motion wasn't completed. He swayed a little. "Try it again," he said.

Bigman tried it again, twisting and diving under his other arm this time and finishing with a little bow to accept the roars of approval.

"Try it again," said Urteil thickly.

"Sure," said Bigman. And he dashed.

This time Urteil was thoroughly prepared. He moved neither head nor arms, but his right foot shot forward.

Bigman doubled, or tried to, in mid-air and didn't quite make it. His ankle was caught and pinned brutally for a moment by Urteil's shoe. Bigman yelped at the pressure.

Urteil's rapid movement carried him forward, and Bigman, with a quick, desperate shove at the other's back, accelerated that movemnt.

This time Urteil, more accustomed to the gravity, was not thrown forward as far and recovered more quickly, while Bigman, with his ankle on fire, moved about with a frightening clumsiness.

With a wild shout Urteil charged and Bigman, pivoting on his good foot, was not fast enough. His right shoulder was caught in one hamlike fist. His right elbow was caught in the other. They went down together.

A groan went up almost in concert from the spectators and Cook, watching ashen-faced, cried out, "Stop the fight" in a croaking voice that went completely unheeded.

Urteil got to his feet, his grip firm on Bigman, lifting the Martian as though he were a feather. Bigman, face twisted in pain, writhed to get a footing of his own.

Urteil muttered into the little fellow's ear. "You thought you were wise, tricking me into fighting under low gravity. Do you still think so?"

Bigman wasted no time in thought. He would have to get at least one foot on the floor. . . . Or on Urteil's kneecap, for his right foot rested momentarily on Urteil's knee and that would have to do.

Bigman pushed down hard and lunged his body backward.

Urteil swayed forward. That was not dangerous for Urteil in itself, but his balancing muscles overshot the mark in the low gravity, and in righting himself he swayed backward. And as he did so, Bigman, expecting that, shifted his weight and pushed hard forward.

Urteil went down so suddenly that the spectators could not see how it was accomplished. Bigman wrenched half free.

He was on his feet like a cat, with his right arm still pinned. Bigman brought his left arm down on Urteil's wrist and brought up his knee sharply against the other's elbow.

Urteil howled and his grip on Bigman loosened as he shifted position to keep his own arm from being broken.

Bigman took his chance with the quickness of a jet's ignition. He wrenched his pinned hand completely loose while maintaining his grip on Urteil's wrist. His freed hand came down upon Urteil's arm above the elbow. He had a two-handed grip now on Urteil's left arm.

Urteil was scrabbling to his feet, and as he did so, Bigman's body bowed and his back muscles went down hard with effort. He lifted along the line of Urteil's own motion of rising.

Bigman's muscles, combined with the action of Urteil's lift, carried that large body free of the ground in a slow motion, impressive display of what could be done in a low gravity field.

With his muscles near to cracking, Bigman whipped Urteil's torso still farther upward, then let go, watching it as it went flailing in a parabolic arc that seemed grotesquely slow by Earth standards.

They all watched and were all caught in the sudden change of gravity. Earth's full gravity snapped on with the force and speed of a blaster bolt, and Bigman went to his knees with a painful wrench on his twisted ankle. The spectators also went down in a chorus of confused cries of pain and astonishment.

Bigman caught only the merest glimpse of what happened to Urteil. The change in gravity had caught him almost at the high point of the parabola, snapping him downward with sharp acceleration. His head struck a protecting stanchion of one of the generators a sharp, cracking blow.

Bigman, rising painfully to his feet, tried to shake sense into his addled brains. He staggered and was aware of Urteil sprawled limply, of Cook kneeling at Urteil's side.

"What happened?" cried Bigman. "What happened to the gravity?"

The others echoed the question. As nearly as Bigman could tell, Cook was the only one on his feet, the only one who seemed to be thinking.

Cook was saying, "Never mind the gravity. It's Urteil."

"Is he hurt?" cried someone.

"Not any more," said Cook, getting up from his kneeling position. "I'm pretty sure he's dead."

They made an uneasy circle about the body.

Bigman said, "Better get Dr. Gardoma." He scarcely heard himself say it. A great thought had come to him.

"There's going to be trouble," said Cook. "You killed him, Bigman."

"The change in gravity did that," said Bigman.

"That'll be hard to explain. You threw him."

Bigman said, "I'll face any trouble. Don't worry."

Cook licked his lips and looked away. "I'll call Gardoma."

Gardoma arrived five minutes later, and the shortness of his examination was proof enough that Cook had been correct.

The physician rose to his feet, wiping his hands on a pocket handkerchief. He said gravely, "Dead. Fractured skull. How did it happen?"

Several spoke at once, but Cook waved them down. He said, "A grudge fight between Bigman and Urteil——"

"Between Bigman and Urteil!" exploded Dr. Gardoma. "Who allowed that? Are you crazy, expecting Bigman to stand up——"

"Easy there," said Bigman. *"I'm* in one piece."

Cook said in angry self-defense, "That's right, Gardoma, it's Urteil that's dead. And it was Bigman who insisted on the fight. You admit that, don't you?"

"I admit it all right," said Bigman. "I also said it was to be under Mercurian gravity."

Dr. Gardoma's eyes opened wide. "Mercurian gravity? Here?" He looked down at his feet as though wondering if his senses were playing him tricks and he were really lighter than he felt.

"It isn't Mercurian gravity any more," said Bigman, "because the pseudo-grav field snapped to full Earth gravity at a crucial time. Bam! Like that! That's what killed Urteil, not yours truly."

"What made the pseudo-grav snap to Earth levels?" asked Gardoma.

There was silence.

Cook said feebly, "It might have been a short——"

"Nuts," said Bigman, "the lever is pulled up. It didn't do that by itself."

There was a new silence and an uneasy one.

One of the technicians cleared his throat and said, "Maybe in the excitement of the fight someone was moving around and shoved it up with his shoulder without even realizing it."

The others agreed eagerly. One of them said, "Space! It just happened!"

Cook said, "I'll have to report the entire incident. Bigman——"

"Well," said the small Martian calmly, "am I under arrest for manslaughter?"

"N—no," said Cook uncertainly. "I won't arrest you, but I have to report, and you may be arrested in the end."

"Uh huh. Well, thanks for the warning." For the first time, since returning from the mines, Bigman found himself thinking of Lucky. This, he thought, is a fine peck of trouble for Lucky to find waiting for him when he comes back.

And yet there was an odd stir of excitement in the little Martian, too, for he was sure he could get out of the trouble ... and show Lucky a thing or two in the process.

A new voice broke in. "Bigman!"

Everyone looked up. It was Peverale, stepping down the ramp that led from the upper levels. "Great Space, Bigman, are you down there? And Cook?" Then almost pettishly, "What's going on?"

No one seemed to be able to say anything at all. The old astronomer's eyes fell on the prone body of Urteil, and he said with mild surprise, "Is he dead?"

To Bigman's astonishment, Peverale seemed to lose interest in that. He didn't even wait for his question to be answered before turning to Bigman once more.

He said, "Where's Lucky Starr?"

Bigman opened his mouth but nothing came out. Finally, he managed to say weakly, "Why do you ask?"

"Is he still in the mines?"

"Well——"

"Or is he on Sun-side?"

"Well——"

"Great Space, man, is he on Sun-side?"

Bigman said, "I want to know why you're asking."

"Mindes," said Peverale impatiently, "is out in his flitter, patrolling the area covered by his cables. He does that sometimes."

"So?"

"So he's either mad or he's correct in saying he's seen Lucky Starr out there."

"Where?" cried Bigman at once.

Dr. Peverale's mouth compressed in disapproval. "Then he *is* out there. That's plain enough. Well, your friend Lucky Starr was apparently in some trouble with a mechanical man, a robot——"

"A robot!"

"And according to Mindes, who has not landed but who is waiting for a party to be sent out, Lucky Starr is dead!"

14

PRELUDE TO A TRIAL

DURING THE MOMENT IN WHICH LUCKY lay bent in the inexorable grip of the robot, he expected momentary death, and when it did not come at once a weak hope flared up within him.

Could it be that the robot, having the impossibility of killing a human being ingrained in its tortured mind, found itself incapable of the actual act now that it was face to face with it?

And then he thought that couldn't be, for it seemed to him the pressure of the robot's grip was increasing in smooth stages.

He cried with what force he could muster, "Release me!" and brought up his one free hand from where it had dragged, trailing in the black grime. There was one last chance, one last, miserably weak chance.

He lifted his hand to the robot's head. He could not turn his head to see, crushed as that was against the robot's chest. His hand slipped along the smooth metal surface of the robot's skull two times, three times, four times. He took his hand away.

There was nothing more he could do.

Then—— Was it his imagination, or did the robot's grip seem to loosen? Was Mercury's big Sun on his side at last?"

"Robot!" he cried.

The robot made a sound, but it was only like gears scraping rustily together.

Its grip *was* loosening. Now was the time to reinforce events by calling what might be left of the Laws of Robotics into play.

Lucky panted, "You may not hurt a human being."

The robot said, "I may not——" haltingly, and without warning fell to the ground.

Its grip was constant, as though rigid in death.

Lucky said, "Robot! Let go!"

Jerkily, the robot loosened his hold. Not entirely, but Lucky's legs came free and his head could move.

He said, "Who ordered you to destroy equipment?"

He no longer feared the robot's wild reaction to that question. He knew that he himself had brought that positronic mind to full disintegration. But in the last stages before final dissolution, perhaps some ragged remnant of the Second Law might hold. He repeated, "Who ordered you to destroy equipment?"

The robot made a blurred sound. "Er—Er——" Then, maddeningly, radio contact broke off, and the robot's mouth opened and closed twice as though, in the ultimate extremity, it were trying to talk by ordinary sound.

After that, nothing.

The robot was dead.

Lucky's own mind, now that the immediate emergency of near-death was over, was wavering and blurred. He lacked the strength to unwind the robot's limbs entirely from his body. His radio controls had been smashed in the robot's hug.

He knew that he must first regain his strength. To do that meant he must get out of the direct radiation of Mercury's big Sun and quickly. That meant reaching the shadow of the near-by ridge, the shadow he had failed to reach during the duel with the robot.

Painfully he doubled his feet beneath him. Painfully he inched his body toward the shadow of the ridge, dragging the robot's weight with him. Again. Again. The process seemed to last forever and the universe shimmered about him.

Again. Again.

There seemed to be no strength or feeling in his legs, and the robot seemed to weigh a thousand pounds.

Even with Mercury's low gravity, the task seemed beyond his weakening strength, and it was sheer will that drove him on.

His head entered the shadow first. Light blanked out. He waited, panting, and then, with an effort that seemed to crack his thigh muscles, he pushed himself along the ground once more and even once more.

He was in the shadow. One of the robot's legs was still in the sun, blazing reflections in all directions. Lucky looked over his shoulder and noted that dizzily. Then, almost gratefully, he let go of consciousness.

There were intervals later when sense perception crawled back.

Then, much later, he lay quietly, conscious of a soft bed under him, trying to bring those intervals back to mind. There were fragmentary pictures in his memory of people approaching, a vague impression of motion in a jet vehicle, of Bigman's voice, shrill and anxious. Then, a trifle more clearly, a physician's ministrations.

After that, a blank again, followed by a sharp memory of Dr. Peverale's courtly voice asking him gentle questions. Lucky remembered answering in connected fashion, so the worst of his ordeal must have been over by then. He opened his eyes.

Dr. Gardoma was looking at him somberly, a hypodermic still in his hand. "How do you feel?" he asked.

Lucky smiled. "How should I feel?"

"Dead, I should think, after what you've gone through. But you have a remarkable constitution, so you'll live."

Bigman, who had been hovering anxiously at the outskirts of Lucky's vision, entered it full now. "No thanks to Mindes for that. Why didn't that mud-brain go down and get Lucky out of there after he spotted the robot's leg? What was he waiting for? He was leaving Lucky to die?"

Dr. Gardoma put away his hypodermic and washed

his hands. With his back to Bigman, he said, "Scott Mindes was convinced Lucky was dead. His only thought was to stay away so that no one could accuse him of being the murderer. He knew he had tried to kill Lucky once before and that others would remember that."

"How could he think that this time? The robot——"

"Mindes isn't himself under pressure these days. He called for help; that was the best he could do."

Lucky said, "Take it easy, Bigman. I was in no danger. I was sleeping it off in the shade, and I'm all right now. What about the robot, Gardoma? Was it salvaged?"

"We've got it in the Dome. The brain is gone, though, quite impossible to study."

"Too bad," said Lucky.

The physician raised his voice. "All right, Bigman, come on. Let him sleep."

"Hey——" began Bigman indignantly.

Lucky at once added, "That's all right, Gardoma. As a matter of fact, I want to speak to him privately."

Dr. Gardoma hesitated, then shrugged. "You need sleep, but I'll give you half an hour. Then he must go."

"He'll go."

As soon as they were alone, Bigman seized Lucky's shoulder and shook it violently. He said in a strangled kind of voice, "You stupid ape. If the heat hadn't got that robot just in time—like in the sub-etherics——"

Lucky smiled mirthlessly. "It wasn't coincidence, Bigman," he said. "If I had waited for a sub-etheric ending, I'd be dead. I had to gimmick the robot."

"How?"

"Its brain case was highly polished. It reflected a large part of the sun's radiation. That meant the temperature of the positronic brain was high enough to ruin its sanity but not high enough to stop it completely. Fortunately, a good part of Mercurian soil about here is made up of a loose black substance. I managed to smear some on its head."

"What did that do?"

"Black absorbs heat, Bigman. It doesn't reflect it. The temperature of the robot's brain went up quickly and it died almost at once. It was close, though. . . . Still, never mind that. What happened at this end while I was gone? Anything?"

"*Anything?* Wow! You listen!" And as Bigman talked, Lucky did listen, with an expression that grew continually graver as the story unfolded.

By the time it drew to a conclusion he was frowning angrily. "Why did you fight Urteil, anyway? That was foolish."

"Lucky," said Bigman in outrage, "it was *strategy!* You always say I just bull right ahead and can't be trusted to do the shrewd thing. *This* was shrewd. I knew I could lick him at low gravity——"

"It seems as though you almost didn't. Your ankle is taped."

"I slipped. Accident. Besides, I *did* win. A deal was involved. He could do a lot of damage to the Council with his lies, but if I won he'd get off our backs."

"Could you take his word for that?"

"Well——" began Bigman, troubled.

Lucky drove on. "You saved his life, you said. He must have known that, and yet that didn't persuade him to abandon his purpose. Did you think he was likely to do so as a result of a fist fight?"

"Well——" said Bigman, again.

"Especially if he lost and would therefore be raging at the humiliation of a public beating. . . . I tell you what, Bigman. You did it because you wanted to beat him and get revenge for making fun of you. Your talk about making a deal was just an excuse to give you an opportunity for the beating. Isn't that right?"

"Aw, Lucky! Sands of Mars——"

"Well, am I wrong?"

"I wanted to make the deal——"

"But mainly you wanted to fight, and now look at the mess."

Bigman's eyes dropped. "I'm sorry."

Lucky relented at once. "Oh, Great Galaxy, Bigman,

I'm not angry at you. I'm angry at myself, really. I misjudged that robot and nearly got myself killed because I wasn't thinking. I could see it was out of order and never tied it up with the effect of heat on its positronic brain till it was nearly too late. . . . Well, the past has a lesson for the future, but otherwise, let's forget it. The question is what to do about the Urteil situation."

Bigman's spirits bounced back at once. "Anyway," he said, "that cobber is off our backs."

"He is," said Lucky, "but what about Senator Swenson?"

"Hmm."

"Ho do we explain things? The Council of Science is being investigated, and as a result of a fight instigated by someone close to the Council, someone who's almost a member, the investigator dies. That won't look good."

"It was an accident. The pseudo-grav field——"

"That won't help us. I'll have to talk to Peverale and——"

Bigman reddened and said hastily, "He's just an old guy. He's not paying any attention to this."

Lucky hitched himself to one elbow. "What do you mean, he's not paying any attention?"

"He isn't," said Bigman vehemently. "He came in with Urteil lying dead on the ground and thought nothing of it. He said, 'Is he dead?' and that's all."

"That's all?"

"That's all. Then he asked about where you were and said Mindes had called and said a robot had killed you."

Lucky's level glance held Bigman. "That's all?"

"That was all," said Bigman uneasily.

"What's happened since then? Come on, Bigman. You don't want me to talk to Peverale. Why not?"

Bigman looked away.

"Come *on,* Bigman."

"Well, I'm being tried or something."

"Tried!"

"Peverale says it's murder and it'll raise a smell back on Earth. He says we've got to fix responsibility."

"All right. When is the trial?"

"Aw, Lucky, I didn't want to tell you. Dr. Gardoma said you weren't to be excited."

"Don't act like a mother hen, Bigman. When is the trial?"

"Tomorrow at two P.M., System Standard Time. But there's nothing to worry about, Lucky."

Lucky said, "Call in Gardoma."

"Why?"

"Do as I say."

Bigman stepped to the door, and when he returned, Dr. Gardoma was with him.

Lucky said, "There's no reason I can't get out of bed by two P.M. tomorrow, is there?"

Dr. Gardoma hesitated. "I'd rather you took more time."

"I don't care what you'd rather. It won't kill me, will it?"

"It wouldn't kill you to get out of bed right now, Mr. Starr," said Dr. Gardoma, offended. "But it's not advisable."

"All right, then. Now you tell Dr. Peverale that I'll be at the trial of Bigman. You know about that, I suppose?"

"I do."

"Everyone does except myself. Is that it?"

"You were in no condition——"

"You tell Dr. Peverale I'll be at that trial and it isn't to start without me."

"I'll tell him," said Gardoma, "and you'd better go to sleep now. Come with me, Bigman."

Bigman squealed. "Just one second." He stepped rapidly to the side of Lucky's bed and said, "Look, Lucky, don't get upset. I've got the whole situation under control."

Lucky's eyebrows lifted.

Bigman, almost bursting with self-importance, said, "I wanted to surprise you, darn it. I can prove I had nothing to do with Urteil breaking his neck. I've solved the case." He pounded his chest. "*I* have. *Me!* Bigman! I know who's responsible for everything."

Lucky said, "Who?"

But Bigman cried instantly, "No! I'm not saying. I want to show you I have more on my mind than fist fights. I'll run the show this time and you watch me, that's all. You'll find out at the trial."

The little Martian wrinkled his face into a delighted grin, executed a small dance step, and followed Dr. Gardoma out of the room, wearing a look of gay triumph.

15

THE TRIAL

LUCKY STRODE INTO DR. PEVERALE'S OFFICE shortly before 2 P.M. the next day.

The others had already gathered. Dr. Peverale, sitting behind an old and crowded desk, nodded pleasantly at him, and Lucky responded with a grave, "Good afternoon, sir."

It was much like the evening of the banquet. Cook was there, of course, looking, as always, nervous and, somehow, gaunt. He sat in a large armchair at Dr. Peverale's right, and Bigman's small body squirmed and was nearly lost in an equally large armchair at the left.

Mindes was there, his thin face twisted glumly and his intertwining fingers separating occasionally to drum on his pants leg. Dr. Gardoma sat next to him, stolid, his heavy eyelids lifting to glance disapprovingly at Lucky as he entered. The department heads among the astronomers were there.

In fact, the only man who had been present at the banquet but was absent now was Urteil.

Dr. Peverale began at once in his gentle way, "We can start now. And first, a few words for Mr. Starr. I understand that Bigman described this proceeding to you as a trial. Please be assured that it is nothing of the sort. If there is to be a trial, and I hope not, it will take place on Earth with qualified judges and legal counsel.

What we are trying to do here is merely to assemble a report for transmission to the Council of Science."

Dr. Peverale arranged some of the helter-skelter of objects on his desk and said, "Let me explain why a full report is necessary. In the first place, as a result of Mr. Starr's daring penetration of the Sun-side, the saboteur who has been upsetting Dr. Mindes's project has been stopped. It turned out to be a robot of Sirian manufacture, which is now no longer functional. Mr. Starr——"

"Yes?" said Lucky.

"The importance of the matter was such that I took the liberty of questioning you when you were first brought in and when your state was one of only half-consciousness."

"I remember that," said Lucky, "quite well."

"Would you confirm some of the answers now, for the record?"

"I will."

"In the first place, are there any other robots involved?"

"The robot did not say, but I do not believe there were others."

"However, it did not say specifically that it was the only robot on Mercury?"

"It did not."

"Then there might be many others."

"I don't think so."

"That's only your own opinion, though. The robot didn't say there were no others."

"It did not."

"Very well, then. How many Sirians were involved?"

"The robot would not say. It had been instructed not to."

"Did it locate the base of the Sirian invaders?"

"It said nothing concerning that. It made no mention of Sirians at all."

"But the robot was of Sirian manufacture, wasn't it?"

"It admitted that."

"Ah." Dr. Peverale smiled humorlessly. "Then it is obvious, I think, that there are Sirians on Mercury and that they are active against us. The Council of Science must be made aware of this. There must be an organized search of Mercury and, if the Sirians evade us and leave the planet, there must at least be an increased awareness of the Sirian danger."

Cook interposed uneasily. "There is also the question of the native Mercurian life-forms, Dr. Peverale. The Council will have to be informed of that, too." He turned to address the gathering at large. "One of the creatures was captured yesterday and——"

The old astronomer interrupted with some annoyance. "Yes, Dr. Cook, the Council shall assuredly be informed. Nevertheless, the Sirian question is what must be kept foremost. Other matters must be sacrificed to the immediate danger. For instance, I suggest that Dr. Mindes abandon his project until Mercury be made safe for Earthmen."

"Hold on, now," cried Mindes quickly. "There's a lot of money and time and effort invested here——"

"I said, until Mercury was safe. I do not imply permanent abandonment of Project Light. And because it is necessary to put the Mercurian danger foremost, it is necessary to make sure that Urteil's protector, Senator Swenson, be prevented from setting up obstructions over side issues."

Lucky said, "You mean you want to present the senator with a scapegoat in the form of Bigman, neatly ticketed and bound hand and foot. Then while he's worrying and clawing at Bigman, the chase for Sirians can proceed on Mercury without interference."

The astronomer lifted his white eyebrows. "A scapegoat, Mr. Starr? We just want the facts."

"Well, go ahead, then," said Bigman, moving restlessly in his chair. "You'll get the facts."

"Good," said Dr. Peverale. "As the central figure, do you care to begin? Tell everything that occurred between you and Urteil in your own words. Tell it in your own words, but I would appreciate brevity. And remember, these proceedings are being recorded on sound microfilm."

Bigman said, "Do you want me to take my oath?"

Peverale shook his head. "This is not a formal trial."

"Suit yourself." And with surprising dispassion, Bigman told the story. Beginning with Urteil's slurs on his height and continuing through the encounter in the mines, he ended with the duel. He left out only Urteil's threats of action against Lucky Starr and the Council.

Dr. Gardoma followed, verifying what had occurred on the occasion of the first meeting between Urteil and Bigman and also describing, for the record, the scene at the banquet table. He went on to describe his treatment of Urteil after the return from the mines.

He said, "He recovered quickly from the hypothermia. I didn't ask him for details, and he didn't offer any. However, he asked after Bigman, and, from his expression when I said Bigman was entirely well, I should judge that his dislike for Bigman was as great as ever. He didn't act as though Bigman had saved his life. Just the same, I must say that from my observation of the man I should say Urteil was not subject to attacks of gratitude."

"That is only an opinion," interposed Dr. Peverale hastily, "and I recommend that we not confuse the record by such statements."

Dr. Cook came next. He concentrated on the duel. He said, "Bigman insisted on the fight. That's all there was to that. It seemed to me that if I arranged one under low gravity as Bigman suggested, with witnesses, no harm would be done. We could intervene if things grew serious. I was afraid that, if I refused, a fight between them might result without witnesses and that there might be serious results. Of course, the results could scarcely be more serious than they have turned out to be, but I never anticipated that. I ought to have consulted you, Dr. Peverale, I admit that."

Dr. Peverale nodded. "You certainly ought to have. But the fact is now that Bigman insisted on the duel and insisted on low gravity, didn't he?"

"That's right."

"And he assured you that he would kill Urteil under those conditions."

"His exact words were that he would 'murder the cobber.' I think he was only speaking figuratively. I'm sure he didn't plan actual murder."

Dr. Peverale turned to Bigman. "Have you any comments in that connection?"

"Yes, I do. And since Dr. Cook is on the stand, I want to cross-examine."

Dr. Peverale looked surprised. "This isn't a trial."

"Listen," said Bigman heatedly. "Urteil's death was no accident. It was murder, and I want a chance to prove that."

The silence that fell at that statement lasted a moment and no more. It was succeeded by a confused babbling.

Bigman's voice rose to a piercing squeal. "I'm set to cross-examine Dr. Hanley Cook."

Lucky Starr said coldly, "I suggest you allow Bigman to go through with this, Dr. Peverale."

The old astronomer was the picture of confusion. "Really, I don't—— Bigman can't——" He stammered himself into silence.

Bigman said, "First, Dr. Cook, how did Urteil come to know the route Lucky and I were taking in the mines?"

Cook reddened. "I didn't know he knew the route."

"He didn't follow us directly. He took a parallel route as though he were intending to catch up and fall behind us well within the mines, after we had convinced ourselves that we were alone and unfollowed. To do that, he would have to be certain of the route we were planning to take. Now Lucky and I planned that route with you and with no one else. Lucky didn't tell Urteil and neither did I. Who did?"

Cook looked wildly about as though for help. "I don't know."

"Isn't it obvious you did?"

"*No*. Maybe he overheard."

"He couldn't overhear marks on a map, Dr. Cook.
. . . Let's pass on, now. I fought Urteil, and if gravity
had stayed at Mercurian normal, he would still be
alive. But it didn't stay there. It was suddenly hopped
up to Earth-levels at just the moment where it helped to
kill him. Who did that?"

"I don't know."

"You were the first one at Urteil's side. What were
you doing? Making sure he was dead?"

"I resent that. Dr. Peverale——" Cook turned a
flaming face toward his chief.

Dr. Peverale said with agitation, "Are you accusing
Dr. Cook of having murdered Urteil?"

Bigman said, "Look. The sudden change in gravity
pulled me to the ground. When I got to my feet,
everyone else was either getting to their feet, too, or was
still on the ground. When 75 to 150 pounds fall on
your back without warning, you don't get to your feet
in a hurry. But Cook had. He was not only on his feet,
he had gotten to Urteil's side and was bending over
him."

"What does that prove?" demanded Cook.

"It proves you didn't go down when the gravity went
up, or you couldn't have gotten there in time. And *why*
didn't you go down when the gravity went up? Because
you *expected* it to go up and were braced for it. And
why did you expect it to go up? Because *you* tripped
the lever."

Cook turned to Dr. Peverale. "This is persecution.
It's madness."

But Dr. Peverale looked at his second in stricken
horror.

Bigman said, "Let me reconstruct the business. Cook
was working with Urteil. That's the only way Urteil
could have learned our route in the mines. But he was
working with Urteil out of fear. Maybe Urteil was
blackmailing him. Anyway, the only way Cook could
get out from under was to kill Urteil. When I said I
could murder the cobber if we fought under low gravity, I must have put an idea into his head, and when we

had the fight he stood there waiting at the lever. That's
all."

"Wait," cried Cook urgently, almost choked, "this is
all—this is all——"

"You don't have to go by me," said Bigman. "If my
theory is right, and I'm sure it is, then Urteil must have
something in writing or on recording or on film that he
can hold over Cook's head. Otherwise, Cook wouldn't
have felt trapped to the point of murder. So search
Urteil's effects. You'll find something and that will be
it."

"I agree with Bigman," said Lucky.

Dr. Peverale said in bewilderment, "I suppose it's the
only way of settling the matter, though how——"

And the air seemed to go out of Dr. Hanley Cook,
leaving him pale, shaken, and helpless. "Wait," he said
weakly, "I'll explain."

And all faces turned toward him.

Hanley Cook's lean cheeks were bathed in perspira-
tion. His hands as he raised them, almost in supplica-
tion, trembled badly. He said, "Urteil came to me
shortly after he arrived on Mercury. He said he was
investigating the Observatory. He said Senator Swenson
had evidence of inefficiency and waste. He said it was
obvious that Dr. Peverale ought to be retired; that he
was an old man and incapable of bearing up under the
responsibility. He said I might make a logical replace-
ment."

Dr. Peverale, who listened to this with an air of
stunned surprise, cried out, "Cook!"

"I agreed with him," said Cook sullenly. "You *are*
too old. I'm running the place anyway while you occu-
py yourself with your Sirius mania." He turned again to
Lucky. "Urteil said that if I helped him in his investigation he would see to it that I would be the next
director. I believed him; everyone knows Senator Swenson is a powerful man.

"I gave him a great deal of information. Some of it
was in writing and signed. He said he needed it for
legal proceedings afterward.

"And then—and then he began holding that written information over my head. It turned out that he was a lot more interested in Project Light and the Council of Science. He wanted me to use my position to become a kind of personal spy for him. He made it quite plain that he would go to Dr. Peverale with evidence of what I had done if I refused. That would have meant the end of my career, of everything.

"I *had* to spy for him. I had to give information concerning the route Starr and Bigman were to take in the mines. I kept him up to date on everything Mindes did. Every time I surrendered a bit more to him I was more helplessly in his power. And after a while I knew that someday he would break me, no matter how much I helped him. He was that kind of man. I began to feel that the only way I could escape was to kill him. If only I knew how——

"Then Bigman came to me with his plan to fight Urteil under low gravity. He was so confident that he could toss Urteil about. I thought then I might—— The chances would be one in a hundred, maybe one in a thousand, but I thought, what was there to lose? So I stood at the pseudo-grav controls and waited my chance. It came and Urteil died. It worked perfectly. I thought it would go down as accident. Even if Bigman were in trouble, then the Council could get him out of it. No one would be hurt except Urteil, and he deserved it a hundred times over. Anyway, that's it."

In the awed silence that followed, Dr. Peverale said huskily, "Under the circumstances, Cook, you will of course consider yourself relieved of all duty and under ar——"

"Hey, hold it, *hold it*," cried Bigman. "The confession isn't complete yet. Look here, Cook, that was the second time you tried to kill Urteil, wasn't it?"

"The second time?" Cook's tragic eyes lifted.

"What about the gimmicked inso-suit? Urteil said for us to watch out for one, so he must have had experience with it. He made out Mindes was doing it, but that Urteil was a lying cobber and nothing he says has to be believed. What I say is that you tried to kill Urteil that way, but he caught the suit and forced you to transfer it to our room when we came. Then he warned us about it just to get us thinking he was on our side and make trouble for Mindes. Isn't that so?"

"No," shouted Cook. "No! I had nothing to do with that inso-suit. Nothing."

"Come on," began Bigman. "We're not going to believe——"

But now Lucky Starr got to his feet. "It's all right, Bigman. Cook had nothing to do with the inso-suit. You can believe him. The man responsible for the slashed inso-suit is the man responsible for the robot."

Bigman stared at his tall friend incredulously. "You mean the Sirians, Lucky?"

"No Sirians," said Lucky. "There are no Sirians on Mercury. There never have been."

16

RESULTS OF THE TRIAL

DR. PEVERALE'S DEEP VOICE was hoarse with dismay. "No Sirians? Do you know what you're saying, Starr?"

"Perfectly." Lucky Starr moved up to Dr. Peverale's desk, sat down on one corner of it, and faced the assemblage. "Dr. Peverale will bear me out on that, I'm sure, when I've explained the reasoning."

"*I'll* bear you out? No fear of that, I assure you," huffed the old astronomer, his face set in an attitude of bitter disapproval. "It is scarcely worth discussing. . . . By the way, we'll have to place Cook under arrest." He half rose.

Lucky urged him gently back into his seat. "It's all right, sir. Bigman will make sure that Cook will remain under control."

"I won't make any trouble," said the despairing Cook in a muffled tone. Bigman pulled his armchair close to Cook's, nevertheless.

Lucky said, "Think back, Dr. Peverale, on the night of the banquet and of your own words concerning the Sirian robots. . . . By the way, Dr. Peverale, you've known for a long time there was a robot on the planet, haven't you?"

The astronomer said uneasily, "What do you mean?"

"Dr. Mindes came to you with stories of having sighted moving manlike figures in what seemed like metal space-suits who also seemed to endure solar radiation better than one would expect humans to."

"I certainly did," interposed Mindes, "and I should have known I was seeing a robot."

"You didn't have the experience with robots that Dr. Peverale did," said Lucky. He turned to the old astronomer again. "I'm sure that you suspected the existence of Sirian-designed robots on the planet as soon as Mindes reported what he had seen. His description fit them perfectly."

The astronomer nodded slowly.

"I, myself," Lucky went on, "did not suspect robots when Mindes told me his story any more than he himself did. After the banquet, however, when, Dr. Peverale, you discussed Sirius and its robots, the thought occurred to me very forcefully that here was the explanation. You must have thought so too."

Dr. Peverale nodded slowly again. He said, "I realized that we ourselves could do nothing against a Sirian incursion. That is why I discouraged Mindes."

(Mindes turned pale at this point and muttered savagely to himself.)

Lucky said, "You never reported to the Council of Science?"

Dr. Peverale hesitated. "I was afraid they wouldn't believe me and that I would only succeed in getting myself replaced. Frankly, I didn't know what to do. It was obvious that I could make no use of Urteil. He was interested only in his own plans. When you came, Starr," his voice grew deeper, more flowing, "I felt I might have an ally at last, and for the first time I felt able to talk about Sirius, its dangers, and its robots."

"Yes," said Lucky, "and do you remember how you described the Sirian affection for their robots? You used the word 'love.' You said the Sirians pampered their robots; they loved them; nothing was too good for them. You said they would regard a robot as worth a hundred Earthmen."

"Of course," said Dr. Peverale. "That's true."

"Then if they loved their robots so much, would they send one of them to Mercury, uninsulated, unadapted to Solar radiation? Would they condemn one of their robots to a slow, torturing death by the Sun?"

Dr. Peverale fell silent, his lower lip trembling.

Lucky said, "I, myself, could scarcely think of blasting the robot even though it endangered my life, and I am no Sirian. Could a Sirian have been so cruel to a robot then?"

"The importance of the mission——" began Dr. Peverale.

"Granted," said Lucky. "I don't say a Sirian wouldn't send a robot to Mercury for purposes of sabotage, but, Great Galaxy, they would have insulated its brain first. Even leaving their love for robots out of account, it's only good sense. They could get more service out of it."

There was a murmur of approval and agreement from the assemblage.

"But," stammered Dr. Peverale, "if not the Sirians then who——"

"Well," said Lucky, "let's see what leads we have. Number one. Twice Mindes spotted the robot, and twice it vanished when Mindes tried to draw close. The robot later informed me that it had been instructed to avoid people. Obviously, it had been warned that Mindes was out searching for the saboteur. Obviously, too, it must have been warned by someone inside the Dome. It wasn't warned against me, because I announced that I was going into the mines.

"Lead number two. As the robot lay dying, I asked once more who had given it its instructions. It could only say, 'Er—er——' Then its radio blanked out, but its mouth moved as though it were making two syllables."

Bigman shouted suddenly, his pale red hair standing on end with passion, "Urteil! The robot was trying to say Urteil! That filthy cobber was the saboteur all the time. It fits in! It fits——"

"Maybe," said Lucky, "maybe! We'll see. It struck me as a possibility that the robot was trying to say, 'Earthman.'"

"And maybe," said Peverale dryly, "it was only a vague sound made by a dying robot and it meant nothing at all."

"Maybe," agreed Lucky. "But now we come to lead number three and it is instantly conclusive. That is this: The robot was of Sirian manufacture, and what human here at the Dome could possibly have had a chance to gain possession of a Sirian robot? Have any of us been on the Sirian planets?"

Dr. Peverale's eyes narrowed. "I have."

"Exactly," said Lucky Starr, "and no one else. That's your answer."

Mad confusion followed and Lucky called for silence. His voice was authoritative and his face stern. "As a Councilman of Science," he said, "I declare this observatory to be in my charge from this moment on. Dr. Peverale is replaced as director. I have been in communication with Council Headquarters on Earth, and a ship is on its way now. Appropriate action will be taken."

"I demand to be heard," cried Dr. Peverale.

"You will be," said Lucky, "but first listen to the case against you. You are the only man here who had the opportunity to steal a Sirian robot. Dr. Cook told us that you were awarded a robot for personal service during your stay on Sirius. Is that correct?"

"Yes, but——"

"You directed him into your own ship when you were through with him. Somehow you managed to evade the Sirians. Probably they never dreamed anyone could commit so horrible a crime, to them, as robot-stealing. They took no precautions against it for that reason, perhaps.

"What's more, it makes sense to suppose the robot was trying to say, 'Earthman' when I asked him who had given it instructions. You were the one Earthman on Sirius. You would be spoken of as 'Earthman' when the robot was first placed in your service, probably. It would think of you as 'Earthman.'

"Finally, who would know better when anyone

might be exploring the Sun-side? Who would better inform the robot by radio when it might be safe and when it ought to go into hiding?"

"I deny everything," said Dr. Peverale tightly.

"There's no point in denying it," said Lucky. "If you insist on your innocence, the Council will have to send to Sirius for information. The robot gave me its serial number as RL-726. If the Sirian authorities say that the robot assigned to you during your stay on Sirius was RL-726 and that it disappeared about the time you left Sirius, that will condemn you.

"Furthermore, your crime of robot-stealing was committed on Sirius, and because we have an extradition treaty with the Sirian planets we may be forced to release you into their custody. I would advise you, Dr. Peverale, to confess and let Earth's justice take its course, rather than to maintain innocence and risk what Sirius might do for your crime of having stolen one of their beloved robots and tortured it to death."

Dr. Peverale stared pitifully at the assemblage with unseeing eyes. Slowly, joint by joint, he collapsed and dropped to the floor.

Dr. Gardoma rushed to his side and felt for his heart. "He's alive," he said, "but I think he'd better be moved to bed."

Two hours later, with Dr. Gardoma and Lucky Starr at his bedside and with Council Headquarters in subetheric contact, Dr. Lance Peverale dictated his confession.

With Mercury falling rapidly behind and the sure knowledge that Council emissaries now had the situation in hand, relieving him of any feeling of responsibility, Lucky still felt tension. His expression was brooding and thoughtful.

Bigman, face puckered anxiously, said, "What's the matter, Lucky?"

"I'm sorry for old Peverale," said Lucky. "He meant well in his way. The Sirians *are* a danger, if not quite as immediate as he thought."

"The Council wouldn't have turned him over to Sirius, would it?"

"Probably not, but his fears of Sirius were sufficiently great to force his confession. It was a cruel trick, but necessary. However patriotic his motives, he had been forced into attempted murder. Cook, too, was goaded into his crime, yet it was none the less a crime, however little we think of Urteil."

Bigman said, "What did the old guy have against Project Light anyway, Lucky?"

"Peverale made that clear at the banquet," said Lucky grimly. "Everything was made clear that night. You remember, he complained that Earth was weakening itself by depending on imported food and resources. He said Project Light would make Earth dependent on space stations for the very manner in which it got its sunlight. He wanted Earth to be self-sufficient so that it could better resist the Sirian danger.

"In his slightly unbalanced mind, he must have thought he would help that self-sufficiency along by trying to sabotage Project Light. Perhaps he originally brought back the robot just as a dramatic demonstration of Sirian power. Finding Project Light in progress when he returned, he turned the robot into a saboteur instead.

"When Urteil arrived he must have been afraid at first that Urteil was going to investigate the Project Light affair and expose him. So he planted a slashed inso-suit in Urteil's room, but Urteil spotted it. Maybe Urteil really believed Mindes had been responsible."

Bigman said, "Sure, come to think of it. The first time we met the old guy he wouldn't even talk about Urteil, he was so mad about him."

"Exactly," said Lucky, "and there was no obvious reason why that should be, as in Mindes's case, for instance. I thought there might be some reason I knew nothing about."

"Is that what put you on to him first, Lucky?"

"No, it was something else. It was the slashed inso-suit in our own room. The man with the best opportunity to do that was obviously Peverale himself. He also would be in the best position to dispose of the suit after it had killed its man. He best knew our assigned room, and he could assign an inso-suit too. What bothered me, though, was the motive? Why should he want to kill me?

"My name apparently meant nothing to him. He asked if I were a sub-temporal engineer like Mindes the first time we met. Now Mindes had recognized my name and tried to get me to help him. Dr. Gardoma had heard of me in connection with the poisonings on Mars. Urteil knew all about me, of course. I wondered if Dr. Peverale might not have heard of me too.

"There was Ceres, for instance, where you and I stayed a while during the battle against the pirates. The largest observatory in the System is there. Might not Dr. Peverale have been there then? I asked him that, and he denied having met me there. He admitted that he visited Ceres, and Cook later told us the old man visited Ceres frequently. Peverale went on to explain, without any prompting from me, that he had been sick in bed during the pirate raid, and Cook later backed that statement. That was the giveaway. In his anxiety, Peverale had talked too much."

The little Martian stared. "I don't get that."

"It's simple. If Peverale had been on Ceres a number of times, how was it he felt it necessary to alibi that particular time when the pirates had attacked? Why that time and not another? Obviously, he knew on which occasion I had been on Ceres and was trying to alibi that one. Obviously, again, he knew who I was.

"If he knew me, why should he try to kill me, and Urteil too? Both of us suffered from slashed inso-suits, you know. We were both investigators. What was it Peverale feared?

"Then he began to talk about Sirians and robots at the banquet table, and things began to drop into place. Mindes's story suddenly made sense, and I knew at once that the only ones who could have brought a robot to Mercury were either Sirians or Dr. Peverale.

To me it seemed that Peverale was the answer, that he was talking about Sirians now as a kind of insurance. If the robot were found and the sabotage stopped, it would serve as a smoke screen to hide his own part and, furthermore, it would make good anti-Sirian propaganda.

"I needed proof. Otherwise, Senator Swenson would shout *we* were setting up a smoke screen to cover the Council's own incompetence and extravagance. I needed good proof. With Urteil right on the ground, I dared not talk about the matter to anyone, Bigman, not even to you."

Bigman groaned in disgust. "When are you going to trust me, Lucky?"

"When I can count on you to avoid tricks like rough-and-tumbles with men twice your size," said Lucky with a smile that robbed the statement of some of its sting. "Anyway, I set out to capture the robot on the Sun-side and use him as evidence. That failed and I was forced to work a confession out of Peverale."

Lucky shook his head.

Bigman said, "What about Swenson now?"

"It's a draw, I think," said Lucky. "He can't do much with Urteil's death, since we can use Dr. Cook as a witness to show some of Urteil's dirty tactics. We can't do much against him, either, since the two top men at the Mercurian Observatory have had to be relieved of duty for felonies. It's a standoff."

"Sands of Mars!" moaned Bigman, "We'll have that cobber on our necks later on then."

But Lucky shook his head. "No, Senator Swenson is not a real cause for worry. He's ruthless and dangerous, but for that very reason he keeps the Council on its toes, keeps us from getting flabby.

"Besides," he added thoughtfully, "the Council of Science needs its critics, just as Congress and the government do. If ever the Council began to consider itself above criticism, then the time might come when it would establish a dictatorship over the Earth, and certainly I wouldn't want that to happen."

"Well, maybe," said Bigman, unsatisfied, "but I don't like that Swenson."

Lucky laughed and reached out to tousle the Martian's hair. "Nor I, but why worry about that now. Out there are the stars, and who knows where we'll be going next week, or why?"

NEL BESTSELLERS

Crime
T012 484 FIVE RED HERRINGS — *Dorothy L. Sayers* 40p
T015 556 MURDER MUST ADVERTISE — *Dorothy L. Sayers* 40p
T014 398 STRIDING FOLLY — *Dorothy L. Sayers* 30p

Fiction
T015 386 THE NORTHERN LIGHT — *A. J. Cronin* 50p
T016 544 THE CITADEL — *A. J. Cronin* 75p
T015 130 THE MONEY MAKER — *John J. McNamara Jr.* 50p
T013 820 THE DREAM MERCHANTS — *Harold Robbins* 75p
T018 105 THE CARPETBAGGERS — *Harold Robbins* 95p
T016 560 WHERE LOVE HAS GONE — *Harold Robbins* 75p
T013 707 THE ADVENTURERS — *Harold Robbins* 80p
T006 743 THE INHERITORS — *Harold Robbins* 60p
T009 467 STILETTO — *Harold Robbins* 30p
T015 289 NEVER LEAVE ME — *Harold Robbins* 40p
T016 579 NEVER LOVE A STRANGER — *Harold Robbins* 75p
T011 798 A STONE FOR DANNY FISHER — *Harold Robbins* 60p
T015 874 79 PARK AVENUE — *Harold Robbins* 60p
T011 461 THE BETSY — *Harold Robbins* 75p
T013 340 SUMMER OF THE RED WOLF — *Morris West* 50p

Historical
T013 758 THE LADY FOR RANSOM — *Alfred Duggan* 40p
T015 297 COUNT BOHEMOND — *Alfred Duggan* 50p
T010 279 MASK OF APOLLO — *Mary Renault* 50p
T014 045 TREASURE OF PLEASANT VALLEY — *Frank Yerby* 35p
T015 602 GILLIAN — *Frank Yerby* 50p

Science Fiction
T015 017 EQUATOR — *Brian Aldiss* 30p
T014 347 SPACE RANGER — *Isaac Asimov* 30p
T015 491 PIRATES OF THE ASTEROIDS — *Isaac Asimov* 30p
T016 331 THE CHESSMEN OF MARS — *Edgar Rice Burroughs* 40p
T013 537 WIZARD OF VENUS — *Edgar Rice Burroughs* 30p
T009 696 GLORY ROAD — *Robert Heinlein* 30p
T016 900 STRANGER IN A STRANGE LAND — *Robert Heinlein* 75p
T011 844 DUNE — *Frank Herbert* 75p
T012 298 DUNE MESSIAH — *Frank Herbert* 40p
T015 211 THE GREEN BRAIN — *Frank Herbert* 30p

War
T013 367 DEVIL'S GUARD — *Robert Elford* 50p
T015 505 THE LAST VOYAGE OF GRAF SPEE — *Michael Powell* 30p
T015 661 JACKALS OF THE REICH — *Ronald Seth* 30p
T012 263 FLEET WITHOUT A FRIEND — *John Vader* 30p

Western
T016 994 No. 1 EDGE – THE LONER — *George G. Gilman* 30p
T016 536 No. 5 EDGE – BLOOD ON SILVER — *George G. Gilman* 30p
T017 621 No. 6 EDGE – THE BLUE, THE GREY AND THE RED — *George G. Gilman* 30p
T014 479 No. 7 EDGE – CALIFORNIA KILLING — *George G. Gilman* 30p
T015 254 No. 8 EDGE – SEVEN OUT OF HELL — *George G. Gilman* 30p
T015 475 No. 9 EDGE – BLOODY SUMMER — *George G. Gilman* 30p

General
T011 763 SEX MANNERS FOR MEN — *Robert Chartham* 30p
W002 531 SEX MANNERS FOR ADVANCED LOVERS — *Robert Chartham* 25p
W002 835 SEX AND THE OVER FORTIES — *Robert Chartham* 30p
T010 732 THE SENSUOUS COUPLE — *Dr. 'C'* 25p

NEL P.O. BOX 11, FALMOUTH, TR10 9EN, CORNWALL
  Please send cheque or postal order. Allow 10p to cover postage and packing on one
book plus 4p for each additional book.

Name ....

Address..

   ....

Title ....
(SEPTEMBER)